ACCIDENT

ACCIDENT

HILA COLMAN

William Morrow and Company
New York   1980

Printed in the United States of America.
1 2 3 4 5 6 7 8 9 10

Library of Congress Cataloging in Publication Data

Colman, Hila.
  Accident.

  Summary: When a motorcycle accident leaves one of them paralyzed, two young people try to cope with feelings of bitterness and guilt.
  [1. Accidents—Fiction. 2. Physically handicapped—Fiction. 3. Friendship—Fiction] I. Title.
PZ7.C7Ac   [Fic]   80-20509
ISBN 0-688-22238-2
ISBN 0-688-32238-7 (lib. bdg.)

ACCIDENT

1

Jenny Melino picked her way along Railroad Street, looking neither to left nor right. She ignored the two habitual drunks on the corner, not even smiling when the older one, Mr. Dibble, bowed low with an elaborate sweep of his arm. On she walked past the used-furniture store, the tobacco shop, a dingy paint store, a small pizza parlor, and the dim entrance to some upstairs apartments, heading straight for her mother's bar and grill. It was known in the village as Louise's place, even though Mrs. Melino did not own it. While most people in Dorchester boasted that their lovely southern Connecticut town with its fine old houses and cared-for lawns didn't have a slum, Louise Melino was one who said, "If Railroad Street isn't a slum, I don't know what is."

The hypocrisy made Mrs. Melino mad. "They pretend Railroad Street isn't here because they don't want to do anything about it," she fumed. "They put flowerpots up on Main Street, but nobody cares about the dirt piling up down here." Jenny was embarrassed sometimes by her mother's vocal anger, especially when Mrs. Melino spoke up at a town meeting and got her name in the newspaper. Who cared about the opinion of a woman who hadn't graduated from high school, lived in a crummy house, and worked nights tending a bar? A woman whose husband had deserted her and left her with two kids, Jenny and her older brother, Mike, to bring up alone?

Besides, Jenny thought that women should have quiet voices and—as she put it to herself bluntly—be refined. She loved her mother and was proud of her in many ways. Louise Melino was handsome when she bothered about her appearance and looked young to have an eighteen-year-old son and a fifteen-year-old daughter. Also, there was no doubt she was a fighter. The last trait was what Jenny floundered on. Her mother said a person had to fight for everything in this world, but Jenny thought that if that was true —and she wasn't sure it was—one had to do so softly, and be important in order to be heard.

That beautiful, sunny May afternoon Jenny's mind and heart were filled with wishes she couldn't put into words. Vague wishes that had to do with spring, yearnings that made her look away from the dreariness of Railroad Street up into the blue sky, fasten her eyes on the light fluffiness of a floating cloud, and wish with all her heart that she didn't have to help her mother in the bar and grill.

Coming from the bright sunshine into the dark bar, Jenny was blinded for a moment and then saw her mother.

The two greeted each other casually. "What do you want me to do?" Jenny asked. "It's so gorgeous out I hate to be inside."

"Yeah, I know." Mrs. Melino looked up from the table she was wiping with a damp sponge. "It'd be more fun to be out roller-skating, wouldn't it?" she said ruefully, and gave Jenny a quick smile.

"It's okay. I'll skate later." Jenny eyed her mother's

round, strong arms, her sleeves rolled up for work, and her lined, good-looking face. "You should let me give you another perm."

"Yeah, one of these days." Mrs. Melino stopped what she was doing and looked up at Jenny.

"What's the matter?"

Her mother smiled, but her eyes looked serious. "You'd like me to look fancier, wouldn't you? Like those ladies you admire. . . ."

Jenny shook her head in embarrassment. "Mom, you're good-looking, but you don't take care of yourself. You can look great when you want to."

"I haven't the time," Mrs. Melino said, wiping her face with her hand. "I'll leave the looks to you. You're growing up to be a beautiful girl, Jenny."

"Oh, Mom. Come on, let's get to work. What do you want me to do?" The question was rhetorical since Jenny knew what to do. She did the exact same thing almost every afternoon unless she had something to keep her at school. In the tiny kitchen in back she sliced bread, spread margarine on one slice and mustard or mayonnaise on another, and piled on ham or bologna or cheese, whatever her mother had in stock. Then she slipped each sandwich into a plastic sandwich bag. Mrs. Melino didn't bother much with food, but she liked to have things for the men to munch on. She believed a little something in the stomach slowed down the process of getting drunk, which was better for business.

Not that many of Mrs. Melino's customers got drunk. She catered to a group of regulars. There wasn't much business at lunchtime, but from about four thirty on she was kept busy serving men who came in on their way home from work. Her customers weren't the professional and business men who lived in the fine houses (they wouldn't be seen in a bar on Railroad Street), but the working men from the factory outside of town, the men who lived in the small, boxlike houses in the new developments.

Jenny could hear them coming in now, greeting her mother, getting their beers or shots of whiskey. It was a good-natured group, yet Jenny deliberately dawdled before bringing out the big platter of sandwiches. Lately she felt ill at ease in the bar for reasons she could not put into words. She didn't like the way the men looked at her. They were rough men, Jenny thought, and sometimes she wished her mother had a different kind of job. Only recently she had asked her, "How do you put up with those guys? All those stupid jokes and the rough talk?"

Mrs. Melino had taken her question seriously. "They're good people, just relaxing after a hard day's

13

work. Better than a lot of those fancy ones with their three-martini lunches. I wouldn't want to serve them. You learn a lot about people in a bar, and anybody says clothes make the man is crazy."

Jenny hadn't been convinced, but she didn't argue. Now she balanced the heaping platter of sandwiches carefully and took it out to deposit on the bar. As she was about to say good-bye to her mother she heard one of the men mention the name De-Witt. So she lingered beside the bar and fussed with the arrangement of the sandwiches. "We was working there all day," the man with the heavy beard was saying. "We fixed one leak in the swimming pool and let the water in, and darn if there wasn't a leak somewheres else. She was fit to be tied, Mrs. DeWitt was. But that boy of hers—Adam they calls him—he ain't stuck up at all. He kept bringing us cold sodas and askin' if he couldn't do something."

"The DeWitt boy's picture was in the paper the other day," one of the other men said. "Says he's goin' to Harvard in the fall. He goes to the public school, don't he?" The man turned to Jenny. "You know him?"

"Sure, I know him. Not well, just to say hello." She wondered what they'd think if they knew she had cut that picture out of the paper and had it folded inside her pocketbook right now.

"You'd think they'd send him to one of them private schools," someone said.

"Not him. He probably wouldn't go," the bearded man replied.

Adam DeWitt and, as a matter of fact, the whole DeWitt family, consisting only of Adam and his parents, were of great interest to Jenny. Her fascination had started one day the past winter. It was a cold, windy, day and Jenny was thumbing a ride home from the shopping mall on the highway. Mrs. DeWitt had picked her up in her Mercedes sports car. She had been chatty, asking where Jenny lived, if she knew Adam in school, if Jenny had plans to go to college, and so forth.

Jenny had answered all the questions: she lived on East Street, the little street off Railroad; she knew Adam by sight; No, she didn't think she was going to college. While she was speaking, Jenny had taken in everything about Mrs. DeWitt—the high, soft leather boots; the fur-lined storm coat; the cashmere gloves; the tense, aristocratic face free of makeup. Jenny thought Mrs. DeWitt was the most refined person she had ever met. Her soft voice and low laugh, the way she drove the car, so easy, so in control, everything about her showed the kind of self-assurance, Jenny thought, that protected a person from the unpleasant, grubby things in life.

Since that day Jenny had been a DeWitt watcher. Her mother and brother didn't know, but she cut out everything in the local papers about the DeWitts: Mr. DeWitt's nomination to a board of directors, Mrs. DeWitt's scores in a golf tournament, or the family's departure on a Caribbean vacation.

Most of all, she was interested in Adam. Some of the kids in school thought he was stuck-up because he kept to himself a lot, but Jenny decided he was shy and, like herself, something of a loner. Besides, he had his photography. That kept him busy. Jenny knew all about his winning first prize at the fair in nearby Small River last fall. She knew, too, that his picture of the big snow had been on the first page of the *Dorchester News*. She sometimes thought of him working in his darkroom and wondered if he ever had a girl there to keep him company. She felt oddly pleased that he was going to Harvard and determined that when she got up her courage she would congratulate him.

Jenny had one good friend, Kate Lacey, an Irish girl who lived in one of the dilapidated wooden houses on East Street, several doors away from the

Melinos. When her chores were over this afternoon, Jenny hurried home to meet Kate. The girls had a date to go roller-skating. The skates had been her mother's big surprise for Christmas, and Jenny had been very moved by the gift. Not only because she knew that skates were expensive, and that her mother must have scrimped to buy them, but that her mother was aware, without Jenny having said a word, how much they would mean to her.

"Short of a motorcycle," Jenny had said, "this is what I wanted the most. They're even better than a cycle. . . ." She hadn't finished the sentence, but she knew before she ever put on the skates that they were going to give her something close to wings—motion, swiftness, power.

Jenny ran upstairs to the converted attic that was her bedroom, a small space with dormer windows and a low, sloping ceiling that she loved. She looked around quickly as she put down her pocketbook, considering whether it was time to repaint. Jenny was constantly redecorating her room. At the moment she had a bright color on one wall, poster and magazine pictures on the others, a much-mended but pretty quilt thrown over her bed, long strands of beads hanging from her mirror. Soon she would be needing fresh paint.

Jenny threw off her shoes, took off her school skirt and blouse, and put on jeans and a sweat shirt. Then she grabbed her skates and went outside to the front steps to put them on. She was tying up her laces when Kate came along on her skates.

"Hi." The girls greeted each other and in a few minutes, without any discussion about where to go, skated off. They headed for their favorite place, which was not far from home, yet seemed to be miles away. When they arrived, Jenny said, as she almost always did, "Isn't this fantastic?"

Stretched ahead as far as they could see was a fine macadam road running alongside a tree-lined river. Since much of the land on both sides of the water was owned by the power company, the road was almost free of houses and, consequently, had little traffic. Here they could let go.

Jenny liked to start off slowly. She let Kate get ahead of her while she savored the fresh smell of the river and the light wind in the trees. Gradually she gathered speed, her legs moving in perfect rhythm, her whole body in tune with her flying feet. Sometimes crouching, sometimes upright, swaying naturally from side to side, she flew down the road, past Kate, past the trees, faster and faster, never out of control, feeling a joy that had no match. Then, at last, she swirled around in a half circle and gracefully came to an abrupt stop.

"This is the greatest," Jenny said with a deep sigh of pleasure, as Kate caught up with her.

The two girls joined hands and with their arms outstretched continued down the road in a comfortable rhythm. Jenny was daydreaming when a motorcycle came zooming around a curve. Kate gave her a yank, and the girls pulled over to the side of the road.

The motorcycle slowed down and came to a stop. Jenny immediately recognized Adam DeWitt. "I'm sorry if I scared you," he said. "I never see anyone on this road."

"We come here all the time," Kate said.

Adam grinned. "Then I guess we come different times."

"I guess we do," Kate agreed.

Adam didn't make any move to go, but sat astride his motorcycle, looking at Jenny. She didn't say a word. "I'm Adam DeWitt," he said finally. "I think I know your name," he added shyly, "Jenny Melino."

"That's right," Jenny said, "and this is my friend Kate Lacey."

"Hi," Adam said. He still looked at Jenny. "My

19

mother said she gave you a lift in her car once."

"That was months ago."

"Yeah, I know. She thought you were very pretty."

Jenny blushed, then got up her courage. "I saw in the paper you're going to Harvard. Congratulations."

"Thanks," Adam said, taking off his goggles.

Jenny could see how bright his blue eyes were against his tanned face.

"Say, would you like to go for a ride?" he asked.

"We couldn't both get on, could we?"

"I guess not. I meant some other time," he said, politely including Kate in his glance.

"Not me." Kate giggled. "I'm scared of those things."

"They're as safe as anything if you know what you're doing," Adam said.

"I'd like to go for a ride sometime," Jenny said, her eyes shining. "The faster the better for me."

"Okay, we'll do it real soon."

The girls were about to take off for home when Adam called, still sitting astride the motorcycle, "Hey, wait a minute."

They turned around to see him holding a camera.

Click, click. "That's not fair," Jenny said, laughing, only to have Adam snap another picture of her.

"Go ahead, skate. Don't pay any attention to me," Adam said. He was off the cycle now, circling around them with his camera in his hands.

"I'll skate so fast you won't see me," Jenny called out, as she skated away from him.

"That's what I want. You look terrific," she heard him answer.

"Boy, he couldn't take his eyes off you," Kate said, when the two girls had slowed down. "Do you think he'll take you for a ride?"

Jenny shrugged. "I don't know. If he doesn't, he doesn't."

Kate laughed. "You're not fooling me. I think you have a crush on him."

"Don't be silly. Even if I did go for a ride with him, it wouldn't mean anything. Can you picture him coming to see me on East Street?"

"Sure. You just fixed up your living room. You said it looked pretty good."

"Pretty good for East Street maybe. Anyway, you know what I mean. Forget it, he'll never ask me."

"I think he will," Kate said.

* * *

21

As he rode along the river on his beloved Honda there was no doubt in Adam DeWitt's mind that he would take Jenny for a ride. He had lied to the girls, a little white lie that didn't hurt anyone. He knew that they skated on this road. Whenever he had seen them there before, he had always turned back because he felt shy. Today had been different. Maybe the news from Harvard or the fact that he had caught Jenny watching him in the students' room the other day had given him confidence. Whatever it was, it had worked, and he felt exhilarated. He had broken the ice. And he had the pictures. He had been dying to get pictures of Jenny on her skates because she looked so wonderful on them.

When Adam had thought about girls in the past, he'd never considered a particular one; his fantasies usually were of some fabulous creature he had yet to meet. That is, until he started to think about Jenny. He wasn't quite sure when the change had begun, but he knew it wasn't long ago. Perhaps it started when he had almost run into her in the hall at school, and she had looked at him with wide, startled eyes, or when he'd seen her walking arm in arm with a tall, dark-haired, broad-shouldered boy and felt an odd sense of relief as he'd realized he was her brother.

Adam rode along the river road whistling. The prospect of having Jenny behind him on the Honda, her arms around his waist, her breath on his neck, was exhilarating. He'd have to plan carefully when to ask her and where they would go. This date had to turn out right.

2

When Jenny got home from skating, she found Mike shooting baskets in the backyard. She sat down on the edge of their picnic table and began to unlace her skates. "That Honda of Adam DeWitt's sure is a beaut," she said.

"Where'd you see him?" Mike turned around, dribbling the ball.

"Down on the river road."

24

"He's a stuck-up punk, the way he rides around showing off on that thing. His father bought it for him." Mike spoke bitterly.

"So what? If you had a father with money you'd be darn glad if he bought you one. You're just jealous."

"Jealous of him? You're nuts! If I really wanted a motorcycle, I could save my money and get one," Mike bragged, speaking with the confidence of one who had an after-school and Saturday job at the supermarket.

Jenny laughed. "You'd have to save for ten years. He's going to take me for a ride on it."

"Did he ask you? When?"

"Sometime. We didn't make a definite date." Jenny gave Mike a defiant look. She was not going to tell him that Adam had taken pictures of her.

Mike scoffed, "I'll believe it when I see it." He dribbled the ball around the table and stopped in front of Jenny. "Stay away from Adam DeWitt. If he goes after a girl like you, he's got only one thing in mind."

Jenny stood up, her face blazing. "What do you mean, a girl like me? What a rotten thing to say to your own sister. I'm as good as any girl in this town and better than a lot. Did it occur to you that if

Adam does want to take me out it might be because he likes me! You are a louse!" Furious, she turned to go into the house.

"Take it easy," Mike called after her. "I wasn't talking about you; I was talking about him. And you know what I mean." He waved his arm toward the block. "You live on East Street, kid, remember, not up on Sunset Hill."

For the next few days Jenny lived with a sense of anticipation. It didn't leave her. She woke up every morning thinking, Will I hear from Adam today? The thought stayed with her as she went through her classes at school, as she walked to the bar to help her mother, as she returned to the river road with Kate. But there was no sign of Adam. "Maybe he's sick," Kate said.

"No, I saw him in school. He waved hello to me, but that was all." Jenny was desolate. So far Mike hadn't said I-told-you-so, but she knew he would sooner or later.

On the fourth day after her meeting with Adam, Jenny was in the students' room looking for a book on the paperback rack. She stood near a group of four or five girls whom she and Kate called the Jet

Set: They were always going someplace and letting everyone in school know about it. It was either the ballet, or the Met (it took Jenny a long time to discover the Met was the Metropolitan Museum of Art), or the theater, or a concert.

She and Kate often made fun of the Jet Set's pretensions to culture, but Jenny also knew she was jealous. She envied their easy familiarity with that privileged world, their knowledge of "the most fabulous painter," the names of the Russian dancers, their ability to distinguish Beethoven from Brahms and Brahms from Mozart. Those girls made Jenny feel inferior, something she did not tolerate easily. "They give me the feeling I'm retarded or something," she confided to Kate. "As if I'm living with a handicap."

In spite of herself, Jenny always was curious to know what the girls were talking about. Now, taking longer than she needed to look for a book, she eavesdropped on their conversation. This time they were talking about going to the Museum of Modern Art Saturday morning and to a concert at Lincoln Center in the afternoon. "My mother said she'd take us to a French restaurant for lunch," a pretty, tall girl named Nancy was saying.

"I'd rather go Japanese. I love the way they cook the food in front of you," Mia, a plump girl with long, blond hair, objected.

"I'll settle the argument," Sharon announced. "We'll go to the Plaza Hotel," she said grandly.

Jenny looked up and caught Sharon's eye. Obviously Jenny had been listening, and all the girls stopped talking to stare at her. After a few seconds of silence, Jenny said, much to her own surprise, "Oh, for heaven's sake, why don't you all just go and have a pizza?"

"Thanks for the suggestion," Sharon said coolly, "but that's something we can always get on Railroad Street."

Jenny gave her a withering glance, smiled sweetly, and said, "Up yours." Then she blindly picked a book from the rack and with deliberate, slow steps walked toward the door. As she reached it, she saw Adam out of the corner of her eye. He was sitting close to where she had been standing and probably had heard the whole conversation.

Damn, Jenny thought. Why did she let those girls get under her skin? Why should she notice them at all, let alone *talk* to them? And, Jenny thought savagely, walking down the hall, that goes for Adam DeWitt, too. He was one of them. She was an idiot to have wasted a moment thinking about him. Where she'd ever gotten the idea he was going to ask her out, or that she wanted to go with him, she didn't know. Adam must be having a good laugh about her right now. If he ever did ask her to go for a ride on that precious Honda of his, she'd tell him to get lost.

Adam hadn't been paying attention to the conversation behind him. Though he knew the girls, he didn't like any of them. To his mind, they were silly and filled with their own importance. They went around seeing a lot of stuff, but he didn't think they understood half of it. The excursions just gave them something to talk about.

But when Adam heard Jenny's voice, he looked around. He hadn't seen her standing there. Interested, he listened closely and had to control his laughter when he heard her response to Sharon. Good for Jenny. More than ever Adam felt that Jenny was a girl he wanted to know better. She seemed so real, so down-to-earth.

In a way she reminded him of Harry Katz, the one friend Adam felt close to. Harry, a Jewish boy, lived near Adam in the grandest house in Dorchester. According to Adam's father, Mr. Katz could buy them all out. The boys had met on the tennis courts, but rarely went out socially. Harry's parents were religious, and most of Harry's social life was connected with activities at the Jewish temple. But the boys visited each other at home, listened to records, sometimes went for walks on the few remaining dirt roads, played tennis, and talked about the world and life.

They didn't see each other at school as Harry was a day student at a private boarding school not far away. "Not my idea," Harry had told Adam, when they first became friends. "My father believes Jews have a harder time in life and have to know more. Maybe he's right."

When Adam got home from school that afternoon, he called Harry. "You feel like getting slaughtered on the court this afternoon?"

"By you, shrimpo?" Harry was about two inches taller than Adam. "Funny, I was just thinking about a couple of six-two, six-three sets I took the other day from a guy who looked a lot like you."

"Must have been somebody else. Are you on?"

"Meet you in fifteen minutes. But do you think you're up to it?" Harry's voice was mischievously solicitous.

"Up to what?"

"Another beating so soon?"

"You'll be dead. Poor Harry, to die so young and so rich. . . . See you." Adam hung up. He felt good. Perhaps life was going to change for him; with Harry, and now Jenny as a friend, he was stepping out on his own, away from the country-club circle of his parents, people he found boring and phony. Like those girls in school.

Adam picked up his racquet and went off to meet Harry.

"I'm in a fighting mood," Adam announced, when the boys took their places on the court. Neither one took their tennis rivalry too seriously, but each played to win. They were fairly well matched, although Harry was slightly stronger.

"Okay," Adam said, after Harry took the first set. "That's just to make you feel good. I'm a generous fellow."

"Especially with your double faults. Damned decent, old man." Harry grinned. He was a tall, lanky boy with horn-rimmed glasses that gave him a wise, professorial look.

Adam took the second set six to four after a few long, drawn-out deuce games, and the boys decided to quit and go for something cold to drink. They walked over to a new ice-cream parlor in town and sat down at a small table and ordered sodas.

"So what's the news on the Rialto?" Harry asked, when they were sipping their sodas.

"Nothing sensational. Except I met a girl I think I like."

"That's pretty sensational for a cynic like you. Tall, blonde, and beautiful, I suppose. And rich, too, I hope."

"Wrong on all counts." Adam grinned. "Not very tall, dark, Spanish looking, beautiful, yes, but not in an ordinary way, and poor. Real poor, I think. I took some pictures of her; I'll show them to you when I develop them."

Harry gave him a questioning look. "What's so great about her?"

"Did I say she was great? Give me time. I haven't even had a date with her yet. But she's real, not a phony like the girls at my parents' club."

"Mmm . . . you mean rich girls are phony and poor ones are for real?"

"Of course not, you boob. Although come to think of it, there may be something in that. Maybe girls— and boys, too, for that matter—who don't have everything aren't spoiled and blasé. Could be, you know."

"Oh, boy, here we go looking for truth and beauty in the slums. I have to take it back. You're not a cynic; you're a romantic. Listen to me, poor people wish they were rich. I think you have ideas about this girl. What's her name, by the way?"

"Jenny. Maybe I do have ideas. So what?"

Harry laughed out loud. "You're not only romantic, you're old-fashioned. You think you have to go to the other side of the tracks to sleep with a girl? Man, I bet every one of those girls at your fancy country club is on the pill."

Adam flushed. "You've got it all wrong. I didn't say anything about sleeping with her, although I wouldn't mind. But that's not it at all. I'm not taking her out because I think she'd be a pushover. And it has nothing to do with whether she's rich or poor. She *is* poor, she lives on East Street, and her mother's a bartender. But you'll see when I show you the pictures. She's alive, nothing artificial, nothing added, no preservatives. She's different from other girls."

Harry looked at Adam with mock sympathy. "Sounds like you got it bad, old man."

"Maybe I have." Adam met Harry's eyes with a

33

sheepish grin. Then he shrugged. "She may not even like me."

"You'd better find out. You going to ask her for a date?"

"You bet."

The boys walked home and said good-bye at Adam's driveway. In his mind Adam went over his conversation with Harry and blushed at the thought that he had any ulterior motive in wanting to take Jenny out. I just like her, he told himself, although the image of her slender body sent his blood racing. Forget it, he muttered, hitting an imaginary ball with a sweeping arc of his racquet. Then he bounded up the path to his house in a wild burst of exuberance.

The next day, after school, Adam rode his motor-cycle over to Louise's place where he knew Jenny spent most of her afternoons. He could see her inside when he parked the Honda. Of course, her mother was there too, and suddenly the thought occurred to Adam that maybe he should have found another place to see Jenny. But it was too late; he was here, and Jenny had already spotted him through the window.

"Hi," he said, when he went inside.

"Hello." Jenny sounded cool. "What brings you here? Going slumming?"

"I thought I could see you for a few minutes." Adam ignored her remark.

"Well, here I am." Jenny turned to her mother and introduced Adam. Then she said in a kinder voice, "Come into the kitchen while I make sandwiches."

Adam turned to follow her through the rear door as Mike came up from the basement. Several cases of beer stood on the floor, and Mike struggled to pick up two, one on top of the other, to carry downstairs. "Let me help you," Adam said, leaning over to take the second case from him.

"Leave it," Mike said brusquely. "I can manage, thank you." He put down the cases and stood upright to face Adam. "You got an ID card? We don't serve minors here."

"I didn't come here for a drink."

"What did you come here for?"

"He came to see me," Jenny said from the doorway. "Come on, Adam." She held the door open for him.

"This ain't a social hall," Mike muttered as Adam

stepped past him to follow Jenny into the kitchen.

"I guess your brother doesn't like me," Adam said with a grin.

"Don't pay any attention to him. But why *did* you come here?" Jenny looked at him suspiciously.

"To see you. To ask if you'd come out with me Saturday night."

"You could have asked me in school. You wanted to see what kind of a hole my mother worked in, didn't you?"

"Don't be ridiculous." Adam flushed. "I can never get hold of you in school. Always so many kids around. I . . . this means a lot to me, Jenny. Will you go out with me?"

Jenny caught his eyes and held them for a minute. He couldn't fathom hers and wondered what she saw in his. Her tone was light when she answered. "Sure, why not? I'll be on the green. You'll find me there."

"Great. I'll see you." He left quickly and not until he was outside did he wonder why she hadn't wanted him to pick her up at her house. He suspected he knew the reason, but he didn't care. The big thing was that he was going to see her on Saturday. Even in that crummy place she had looked terrific. Adam liked to think of her best on her roller skates, the way she raced along, swift and graceful, action on the move. Grinning to himself, he decided to get to work on those pictures as soon as he got home.

3

Jenny usually went to the green on Saturday nights because there was nothing else to do. The talk in town was that soon the kids weren't even going to be allowed to gather on the green. Could make for vandalism, people said. According to Louise, "the 'people' were the ones whose kids had money for theaters and discos."

But on this Saturday night Jenny's spirits were

high. She was humming her favorite tune as she brushed her hair before going out. Adam and the Honda. Maybe he wouldn't show . . . but of course he would. He said they had a date. She was not going to worry about his not coming. Tonight was their first date; it was only the beginning. Her fantasies raced ahead: Adam and Jenny riding everywhere together, Adam and Jenny going hiking, Adam and Jenny going to the movies, going swimming in his pool, Jenny visiting Adam at Harvard. . . . She looked at herself in the mirror and grinned. "You are a crazy girl," she said. "You got no money, you can't afford a college education, you're just a little speck of nobody. You'll be lucky if Adam DeWitt takes you for a puny little ride tonight on his machine." But she kept on humming.

"What are you feeling so good about?" Mike was standing in the doorway of her room. Jenny looked at her brother. Although he was taller and broader, they could pass for twins. They had the same olive complexion and high cheekbones, the same wide-set hazel eyes with long black eyelashes that matched their jet-black hair.

"Nothing. I just feel happy."

"You going to meet that punk Adam DeWitt?"

Jenny continued brushing her hair, but she gave

her brother a withering look. "He's not a punk. You don't know him. Besides, I'm meeting everyone."

"He thinks he's so big with that Honda of his. He's a stuck-up punk."

"Lay off, will you? You're jealous, that's all. You wish you had his money. And his brains. He's going to Harvard in the fall."

"So what? I bet his father bought his way in."

Jenny put down her hairbrush. "You're a jackass. You can't buy your way into Harvard. Don't show your ignorance."

"You can buy your way into anything. Anyway, take my advice and don't get mixed up with him. I told you, he's out for just one thing with a girl like you."

Jenny's eyes blazed. "Stop saying that! You've got a dirty mind. Don't judge others by yourself."

Jenny heard the front door slam behind Mike. Mike could make her angrier than anyone in the world. Damn him for putting into words a vague uneasiness she herself felt. What *was* in Adam's mind? He had his own crowd; why suddenly did he want to take out Jenny Melino, whose mother worked in a crummy bar?

Jenny stopped to examine herself in the mirror.

She was wearing a white sweater of her mother's that accentuated her curves, and she felt the same wave of self-consciousness that she did when the men in the bar looked at her. Okay, so she looked sexy. That was nothing to be ashamed of. If Adam had any ideas about her, he'd soon find out he was wrong. She wasn't worried. Adam had beautiful manners, and she was sure he was a gentleman. After all, that was what she liked best about him.

After one last look in the mirror, Jenny went downstairs and walked along her street of small, frame houses. Most of them needed painting. She waved hello to the kids playing in their front yards and the grandparents on their rockers, but her mind was on Adam.

Some of Jenny's friends were already sitting on the grass near the Civil War cannon: Kate and her boyfriend, Roger, Roger's sister, Anna, and three or four other kids from school. Jenny greeted them and sat down next to Kate.

"You look pretty tonight," Kate remarked.

"Thanks. I'm wearing my mother's sweater." Jenny's eyes kept darting to Willis Street, the direction Adam would be coming from. She wondered if he was really going to show up.

"Let's go for a walk," Roger said. "Sitting here is boring."

"Okay," Kate agreed. She stood up. "Come on, Jenny. You're included."

"You two go. I don't feel like walking."

Kate looked at her inquiringly. "You waiting for someone?"

"Maybe."

"You don't have to tell me who." Kate had a knowing smile. "Should we come back and get you if we go for pizza?"

Jenny hesitated. Was Adam going to show or not? "No, don't bother. Maybe I'll walk over and meet you later. But don't wait for me."

Kate grinned. "Have a good time."

Jenny moved closer to Anna and the others, but she wasn't paying attention to their conversation. Her ears strained to pick up the whir of a motorcycle. Then, a short while after Kate and Roger had left, Adam appeared. Jenny's heart beat faster as he parked his motorcycle and came over to her. He looked terrific in his helmet, thin, black jacket, and corduroy jeans.

"Hi," he said to the group. He took hold of her hands and pulled her up from the grass. "Sorry if I'm late." He spoke softly to Jenny.

42

"You're not late. There was no definite time."

"Wasn't there? I'd have been mad if you weren't here. I've been looking forward all day to seeing you."

Jenny laughed. "Well, here I am."

"Come on." He was still holding one of her hands. "Let's go somewhere."

"Where?" Jenny walked along with him toward the motorcycle.

"I don't know. We'll find a place."

Jenny felt excited. This evening was not going to be just another Saturday night of hanging around, going for a walk, having a pizza. . . . Mike was all wrong. Adam wasn't faking; he liked her. She could tell. And she liked him. To have him kiss her might be very nice.

Jenny settled herself behind Adam on the motor-cycle and put her arms around his waist. "Hold on tight," he said, and they were off. They moved slowly until they left the center of town, then speeded up as they reached the outskirts. When they approached the highway, Adam slowed down almost to a stop.

"Shouldn't I have a helmet?" Jenny called to him.

"Yes, I'm sorry. I forgot. We'll have to go back to my house to get one." There was a question in his voice.

"Don't bother. I'll be okay." Adam lived way out on the other side of town. Going back to his house would be a drag.

"I'm careful. We're not going far anyway."

"Where are we going?"

"I thought the lake. It's pretty this time of year. Nobody's there. Okay?"

"Sure." Jenny wriggled in her seat. She could feel the warmth of Adam's body against her, and her sense of anticipation and excitement made her tingly. It had gotten dark, and the first stars were showing. Adam revved up the motor, and they flew down the highway. Jenny thought that this moment was the greatest in her life. It was even better than she had imagined. Every nerve in her body had come to life, and she felt that if she wanted she could reach out and touch the stars.

Adam left the blacktop and swerved the Honda gracefully onto the gravelled lake road. He followed the curves, the machine noisily spitting out pieces of gravel. The motorcycle was careening wildly. "Hey, what are you doing?" Jenny called out as the Honda swerved from one side of the road to the other.

"Trying to avoid the holes," Adam answered.

Soon the road became a narrow dirt path. After

a short while Adam pulled the motorcycle over to a stop.

"You okay?" He jumped off and offered Jenny a hand.

"Sure, I'm fine. Where are we?"

"You'll see," he said, still holding her hand.

"I can't see much. It's pretty dark."

"Just follow me." Adam led her down a path, about a hundred yards, until the lake suddenly appeared in front of them. The sky had become lighter, and a misty half-moon gave the lake and the dark outline of trees along its edge an eerie light. Adam led her to a large, flat-topped rock that jutted out over the water.

"Isn't it pretty here?" he asked.

"It's beautiful. How did you ever find this place?" Jenny sat down beside him on the rock.

"We used to swim here when I was a kid. My father had a boat, and he liked to fish from this rock. He'd fish and I'd swim."

"That sounds nice." Jenny sighed. "I don't know my father. He left home when I was a baby. Can you imagine a man leaving his wife and two babies, just like that? Just going off one day and not coming back? What a louse. I don't think of him much, but when I do, I get mad. I hate him."

"Maybe he had a reason," Adam said.

Jenny laughed. "Sure he had a reason. He didn't want to support us. Mom says he never kept a job more than a few weeks; he'd always find something wrong and quit."

"It must have been tough for your mother."

Jenny looked up at Adam. "Yeah, it was. I don't know why I'm telling you all this. You're not interested in my family history." Jenny picked up a pebble and tossed it into the lake.

"I'm interested in everything about you," Adam said quietly, moving closer to her. "Why does your brother dislike me so much?" he asked abruptly.

Jenny edged a little away from him. "I don't know." Then she laughed. "I do know, but it's stupid. Don't pay any attention to Mike."

"But I want to know." Adam took hold of Jenny's hand again. "Tell me, please."

"It's stupid, honestly." Her eyes met his, but he was looking at her so intently that she turned her face away. She felt a sincerity in him that made her ashamed of repeating Mike's thoughts. Mike didn't know anything about a boy like Adam. Jenny was positive Adam would never touch a girl unless he really liked her. "Oh, Mike had some cuckoo idea you wanted to take me out just to . . . oh, you know, just to make out. I told you it was stupid," she added quickly. She took a swift look at his face and was startled by the anger in it.

"What a lousy thing to say," Adam said. "Did you think that, too?"

"Of course not. I wouldn't be here if I did. Forget Mike, please." Jenny moved closer to him and turned her face to his. She felt mischievous. "I think it would be nice if you kissed me."

Adam laughed. "You're too smart. You know that after what you just said I could never ask you."

"That's right," Jenny said with a grin.

Adam bent down and kissed her lightly on her mouth. They pulled away so that they could see each other's face. "To hell with Mike," Adam said, and he took Jenny in his arms and kissed her mouth, her cheeks, her eyes. They held each other tight.

When finally they let go they sat quietly side by side. Jenny drew her knees up and wrapped her arms around them. Adam sprawled out beside her, his feet just over the edge. Neither of them spoke for several minutes.

"Have you been here with a girl before?" Jenny broke the silence.

Adam turned to face her. "No. I was saving it. I'm glad I did."

"So am I," Jenny said. "I wish I could stay much longer, but I think we'd better go now."

"Not yet. Let's sit here awhile. Jenny"—he reached out and took her hand—"this is pretty important to me. It's nothing casual. You know what I mean?"

"I think so. But, well . . . let's see what happens."

"What are you afraid of?"

"I'm not afraid, just cautious. I guess I'm a realist."

"And I'm a romantic?" Adam laughed. "That should make a good combination, shouldn't it?"

"We'll see."

Adam shook his head impatiently. "You don't trust me? Your brother's brainwashed you, hasn't he?"

Jenny stood up. "I think we should go."

"Okay." Adam got up, and before they left the rock he gave her a long, sweet kiss.

Jenny got on the motorcycle behind him and put her arms around his waist. She felt wonderfully happy, although afraid to admit to herself, or to Adam, how happy she was. Holding on to him now, encircling his body in her grasp, resting her face against his shoulder, she felt part of a whole. Jenny and Adam . . . Jenny Melino and Adam De-Witt. . . . Jenny laughed softly to herself.

The warm aura of pleasure was suddenly pierced by a sharp pain in her right eye. "Ouch!" she yelled. "Something hit me. . . ." Automatically she let go of Adam to rub her eye, barely hearing Adam's voice as the motorcycle seemed to leave the ground and go soaring into the air.

"Hang on," Adam was yelling. "We're going to hit this one. . . ."

Jenny's arms were flailing in the air, and she could find nothing to grab. There was no time . . . she felt herself being flung into the air and did not even see the rocky ground where she landed.

Adam stopped the motorcycle and hastily swung off. "Jenny," he called into the darkness. "Jenny, you okay?" His only answer was the hoarse croaking of a frog in the lake. "Jenny, c'mon. Come out, come out, wherever you are," he sang facetiously. "Damn!" Adam groped his way into the bushes and caught his slacks on some thorns. "Jenny, please, don't play games now. Where are you?"

An uneasy fear was rising in Adam that made his tone impatient. "Jenny . . . Jenny. . . ." The sound of his voice in the empty night frightened him. "Jenny," Adam called again.

There was no answer. He stumbled through the

thorny bushes until he came to where Jenny lay sprawled on her back, her slender arms flung wide, her face pale. If her eyes had been open, she might have been stargazing. But her eyes were closed, and as Adam stared down at her he thought how uncomfortable she looked; no one would choose to lie that way. "Jenny. . . ." He bent down and listened for her heartbeat. She was breathing. He took off his jacket and was about to put it under her head when he remembered something he'd heard about not moving anyone who had been hurt. Instead, he covered her with the jacket and looked at her, willing that she open her eyes. But she didn't. Still, he kept staring at her, beseeching her to respond. He could not believe that she wouldn't.

Adam felt torn between not wanting to leave Jenny alone (What if she came to there in the dark?) and knowing that he had to go for help. After several minutes he reluctantly left and raced up the road, his head spinning.

Mr. and Mrs. Emanuel Cohen, a retired couple in their sixties, were watching a rerun of "All in the Family" when their doorbell rang. "Don't answer it," Mrs. Cohen said. "We're not expecting anyone."

She felt uneasy until the summer people came and their stretch of road wasn't so lonely.

"I'll look before I open the door," her husband said.

He wasn't much reassured by the sight of a tall young man wearing a helmet, an open shirt, and no jacket on a chilly night. Through the glass door the boy's voice was tense and pleading. "Please, I need to use the phone. There's been an accident."

"Who do you want to call?"

"The hospital for an ambulance."

"Someone hurt?"

"Yes, please, hurry up. You can call. I'll wait out here."

"You can come in if you want," Mr. Cohen said in a kinder voice, and he opened the door.

Inside the warm house Adam felt himself shaking. "I covered her with my jacket, but I don't like leaving her there alone. I'd better go back. Tell the ambulance we're about fifty yards below your house. They'll see my motorcycle by the road. Tell them to hurry, please."

"I'll come down after I call," Mr. Cohen said.

The two paramedics on the ambulance were gen-

51

tle and expert as they examined Jenny for vital signs. But their casual words were chilling to Adam. "We've got to keep her rigid on the stretcher. For all we know she could have a broken spine or a broken neck. Looks like a bad job."

"Heart's okay, breathing okay," the short one said.

"Right. I'll keep the oxygen handy anyway. Here come the cops."

The police car drew up, and two officers got out. They came up to Adam. "You the owner of this vehicle?" one of them asked, motioning to the motor-cycle.

"Yes, sir, I am."

His eyes kept going to the medics, who were carefully sliding the stretcher under Jenny's inert body. He could hear their directions to each other. "Keep her level . . . here, this way. . . ."

"Let's see your license."

"My wallet's in my jacket pocket. It's . . . it's on the girl."

"Go get it."

Gingerly he lifted his jacket from where he had spread it out over Jenny's stomach. The blood and scratches on her face did not hide the pallor underneath. "Is she going to be all right?" Adam asked the ambulance men.

"No way of knowing," came the brief reply.

"She's young. She'll be all right," Mr. Cohen said. He had waited with Adam for the ambulance.

"Don't count on it," the medic said. "You should see some of the kids we pick up from motorcycle accidents. You couldn't pay me to ride one of those things. They're killers."

Adam walked back to the cops. He showed them his license and his insurance identification card.

"Tell us what happened."

Adam took a deep breath and cleared his throat nervously. "She called out that a piece of dirt hit her. Maybe it got in her eye. Anyway, she let go of me, and the next thing I knew we hit a hole in the road and she was flying off. If she hadn't let go, nothing would have happened. I was yelling for her to hang on."

"Was she wearing a helmet?"

"No, sir."

"What about goggles? Did she have anything over her eyes?"

"The law doesn't require them."

"I know all about the law." The officer's face was grim. "You wear them, don't you? And a helmet, too, I notice. Don't you think it would have been a good idea for her?"

"Yes, sir."

Adam was asked a few more questions and then told he could go. The ambulance had already left with Jenny.

"Maybe you should call the girl's parents." Mr. Cohen spoke in a kind voice. He had stood by while the officer was questioning Adam. Now they both watched the police car drive off.

"Her mother works nights. She hasn't got a father. . . ." Adam looked dazed. "I've got to get to the hospital."

"You want me to go with you?"

Adam gave Mr. Cohen a grateful look. "That's very kind of you, but I'll be okay. I haven't a scratch on me. If that hole hadn't been there. If I'd only seen it sooner. Why did she have to let go just that minute? God, if anything happens to her. . . ."

"She'll be all right. Probably just a few bumps and bruises."

"You think so?" Adam looked at the old man eagerly. "They said her vital signs were okay. But she looked so pale. I had to make sure she was breathing. I've got to go. Thanks for everything. You've been great." He shook the old man's hand hurriedly, picked the Honda up off its side, and took off.

Back on his motorcycle, Adam felt shaky, but he kept repeating that Jenny would be all right. That old man knew more than he did about things like that. Even the medics had seemed casual. If someone was dying or even badly hurt, they'd have acted differently. As Mr. Cohen had said, Jenny was young and strong. . . .

4

At midnight Louise Melino had been sitting outside the emergency room of the Dorchester Hospital for about two hours. All she knew was that her daughter had been thrown from a motorcycle, that she was unconscious, and that so far the X rays had not shown any spine or neck injuries.

Mrs. Melino stood up as the heavy door of the emergency room opened. "We don't know why she is unconscious," Dr. Farnum, the Melino family physician, told her. She had called him as soon as she'd heard about the accident. "Her vital signs are all right, her heart is okay, her breathing's a little hard, but nothing to be alarmed about as yet. . . ."

"Why doesn't she come to? There's got to be a reason." Mrs. Melino studied the doctor's face. Was he keeping something back?

"We're taking X rays of her entire body—pelvis, arms, legs. We've tested for internal bleeding. There isn't any. She wasn't on any drugs, was she?"

Mrs. Melino shook her head vigorously. "No, not Jenny. I'll vouch for that."

"If you want to go home, I'll call you the minute we know anything. Or if she wakes up." Dr. Farnum looked at her sympathetically.

"I'm not budging from this place until my Jenny is conscious and we know what happened. You're not keeping anything from me, are you?"

"Of course not. You know better than that. Where's Mike?"

"I've left messages for him everyplace. He'll show up soon."

Dr. Farnum glanced over at Adam, who was sitting by himself, his elbows resting on his knees, his head in his hands. "Is the boy staying, too?"

"I don't know. Ask him. Damn fool kid, I wish Jenny'd never laid eyes on him. I can't help feeling sorry for him, though. I don't need him to look at, but I haven't the heart to tell him to go home."

Dr. Farnum spoke to Adam in a low voice and disappeared again into the emergency room.

The woman and the boy sat in silence, Adam with his head down, Mrs. Melino's eyes restlessly roving the room, coming back to the door every few minutes. She had seen Jenny when she'd first arrived, and the image of her small, pale face was fixed, she believed forever, in her mind.

Around one o'clock Mike showed up, Kate and Roger with him. He strode into the waiting room and went directly to his mother. "What happened?"

Briefly Mrs. Melino told him all she knew about the accident. "Jenny's unconscious. They don't know why. . . . It's not her back, and it's not her neck. Thank God for that. They're taking more tests. We'll just have to wait."

Kate and Roger sat down beside Mrs. Melino. Mike spun around and stood in front of Adam. "We don't need you here. You can go home."

Adam looked up at the angry face above him. "I'll stay here if you don't mind."

"I do mind." Mike's arms were by his side, but his fists were clenched.

"I'm not taking orders from you. I'm staying here." Adam's voice rose.

Mike made a move as if to punch him. "Mike, cut it out." Mrs. Melino jumped up from her seat. "Your sister may be dying! You're not going to have a fight here. Adam has a right to stay if he wants."

"He has *no* right! He doesn't give a damn about Jenny. If he did, he wouldn't have let her on that machine of his unprotected—no helmet, nothing over her eyes. I don't want to have to look at him! I'm telling you, he'd better get out of here or I'll kill him. . . . What the hell was he doing with her on that lake road anyhow?"

Adam stood up and spoke in a tired voice. "I can't blame you for being upset. She's your sister. I don't want your mother bothered any more than she is already, so I'll leave. But as soon as Jenny can see me, I'm going to visit her, and you're not going to stop me." Adam picked up his jacket and helmet from a chair, nodded good-bye to Mrs. Melino and walked out.

"That boy's a gentleman," Mrs. Melino said after he'd left. "You gotta admit that."

"He's a punk. If I see him around here again, he's had it."

"Let's not have any more trouble than we've got already." Mrs. Melino patted his shoulder soothingly as if he were an infant. Mike gave her a weak smile, but his face resumed its scowl as he pulled out a chair and sat down heavily.

The three young people and Mrs. Melino sat in silence. Once Kate murmured, "She looked so pretty tonight. She said she was wearing your sweater. . . ." Then she burst into tears, and Roger put his arms around her. Mike got up and paced around the room while Mrs. Melino continued to sit quietly alert as if she were expecting to hear her daughter's voice at any moment.

The sun was above the horizon when Dr. Farnum came in to say that the medical team wanted to call in a consultant neurologist. "We all agree on Dr. Steinberg. Our neurologist, Dr. Fine, is a good man, but he would like another opinion. Is that all right with you, Louise?"

"Of course. Whatever you say. What do you think it is? What are you looking for?"

"A fall like the one Jenny had is bound to result in some head injuries. We want to pinpoint exactly where they are."

"Is she . . . are you telling me her brain is affected, that she'll be . . . ?" Mrs. Melino couldn't say the incredible word that had formed in her mind.

"I'm not saying anything. We don't know. It's very difficult to make a neurological diagnosis of someone who is unconscious and can't give us meaningful reactions. I know it's hard on you, but there's little to do but wait and see. We're going to move her out of emergency up into the intensive-care unit. We can monitor her heart and breathing better there. Don't be alarmed, but we may decide to do a tracheotomy."

"What's that?" Mrs. Melino asked sharply.

"It's not as bad as it sounds." Dr. Farnum looked at her with kind eyes. "It's a small incision in the throat to make her breathing easier."

"You mean you're going to cut her throat?" Mike asked incredulously.

"Take it easy, boy. We're doing everything we can. Don't forget, I've known Jenny since she was born."

"Of course, I know that. I know you're doing everything." Mrs. Melino held Mike's hand tightly, and her eyes filled with tears. "Mike'll be all right. He loves Jenny very much. We all do. I guess all we can do is pray. . . ."

Mrs. Melino sat down and pulled Mike down beside her. She kept a tight hold of his hand until she saw his face relax.

All through the day Mrs. Melino and Mike kept their vigil in the hospital. They moved from the waiting room near the emergency room to one on the floor that held the intensive-care unit. Occasionally one or the other took a catnap. Mike went down to the cafeteria several times and brought back coffee and sandwiches. Twice they accompanied one of the nurses in to see Jenny. Mrs. Melino wanted to bend down and kiss her, but she was afraid. Perhaps someone in intensive care had to be protected from any chance of outside infection. She looked at Mike. He was pale, and sweat covered his face.

"She looks like a piece of machinery with all those tubes sticking out of her," he said.

A second night passed, and by the second day Mrs. Melino had lost all track of time. She thought they'd been sitting there at least three or four days. Various friends came to see them; Mrs. Melino's boss, the owner of the bar, brought hot pastrami sandwiches, which she loved. She tried to eat one to please him, but she could only manage a half. Kate and Roger came back, along with other friends of Mike and Jenny. Neighbors on their block came. Some said they were saying a mass for Jenny; some brought fruit and cookies. The Melinos were not churchgoers, but the parish priest came as well as the rabbi from the synagogue where Louise Melino sometimes helped at catered affairs. Everyone knew Jenny.

Mrs. Melino was grateful for the concern of their friends, but she was frightened by certain veiled hints and unspoken condolences. "Mrs. Jarowski thinks Jenny is going to be a vegetable—if she lives," she said to Mike after one visit.

"What does Mrs. Jarowski know? She's an idiot. She doesn't know a damn thing. Don't pay attention, Mom. Did that fool say that?" he asked as an after-thought.

"Not exactly, but I know that's what she thinks. So do some of the others. Head injuries. That's brain damage, isn't it?"

"I don't know. People can get terrible cracks on the head and be all right. Don't think about it. Forget Mrs. Jarowski."

"I don't care what she's got. I want her to live. I'll take care of her. Even if—well, even if she's not a hundred percent all right."

"Cut it out, Mom. She's going to be all right." Mike bit his lip.

On the third day, Mr. Cohen stopped by. "The

boy called the ambulance from my house," he explained. "I don't want to disturb you, but I'd like to know how the little girl is?"

"We don't know yet. She's in a coma." Mrs. Melino had never said the word out loud before, and for the first time she began to cry. "It was so kind of you to come. . . ." She wanted Mr. Cohen to think she was crying because she was moved by his concern.

"She'll be all right," Mr. Cohen said soothingly. "And the boy? He was so upset. . . ."

"He damn well should be," Mike said harshly.

Mr. Cohen looked at Mike with understanding. "It was an accident. Don't be hard on the boy. He's suffering, too."

That same evening another man came into the waiting room and without hesitation walked over to Mrs. Melino. "I'm Adam's father," he said. "John DeWitt. I don't want to intrude, but I'd like you to know we are very concerned." He was a tall, nervous man who moved uneasily. His voice was low, and he spoke with a marked Boston accent.

"Thank you," Mrs. Melino murmured. She glanced at Mike anxiously.

"I—I hope you don't take this the wrong way, but

as far as expenses are concerned. . . . Well, don't spare anything. We would like to take care of the bills. Not that we think it was Adam's fault. It was. . . ."

"It *was* his fault," Mike cut him short. "It was his goddamn fault!"

"Mike, please. Thank you, Mr. DeWitt. I haven't given any thought to money. I think we can take care of Jenny ourselves. It was nice of you to come." Mrs. Melino lowered her head. She was not going to break up again, not in front of him.

Mr. DeWitt stood in front of her for a few minutes, then gave Mike a nervous glance, and turned and left.

"Good riddance to him," Mike said, and ran his hands through his thick, rumpled hair. "Him and his son. If I see either one of them again, it's gonna be too soon."

Adam was sick. He had no appetite, and if he did make an attempt to swallow something, he couldn't keep it down. "You must have picked up a bug," his mother said.

"Yeah," Adam agreed. But he didn't think so. He was sick with thinking about Jenny. Perhaps the worst part was being cut off, not knowing if she was dead or alive. He told himself, however, that if she had died, he would have heard about it.

He had stayed home from school for a day, but that was no good either. He didn't want to see anyone in school, but he did want to be there to get some news.

As he expected, the school was buzzing about the accident. To Adam's surprise, however, no one bothered him. Being ignored was nothing new for him, and if some conversations stopped when he approached, he didn't care.

Then, as he was leaving school in the afternoon, Kate, Jenny's friend, came over to him. "Adam, I'm sorry," she said. "I don't know what happened—you hear all kinds of rumors—but I'm sure it wasn't your fault."

"It wasn't. I swear it wasn't," Adam said eagerly. "It was an accident, a stupid, awful, accident. How is Jenny? Tell me. What do the doctors say?"

"I don't think they're saying anything much yet. She's still unconscious . . ."

Adam stood quite still. "If anything happens to her, I—Oh God, I can't even think about it."

Kate put her hand on his arm. "Don't. We're all

praying for her. That's all we can do, I guess. Take it easy."

Adam thanked her and said good-bye. He hadn't ridden the Honda since the accident, and he didn't feel like taking the bus. Instead he began to walk aimlessly and wandered into the village. He thought of Jenny and Kate roller-skating, and waves of nausea hit him again. With effort Adam fought the feeling back, afraid he would get sick on the street.

He kept thinking about the pictures he had taken of the girls. He had planned to develop them the previous Sunday, the day after the accident, but he hadn't been able to face looking at them. In fact, he had been tempted to destroy the film, but he couldn't do that either. The roll of film was still sitting in his darkroom.

Now the idea struck him of going to see Mr. Cohen. He had thought about calling to thank him for being so decent the night of the accident, and he decided it would be a nice gesture to stop in to see him. There was also another reason; it would give him a chance to talk about Jenny. God, Adam thought, I must be going bananas to think of Mr. Cohen, a stranger, as a link to Jenny.

Adam headed out toward the lake road, but almost

turned back when he got there. He thought of the saying that a murderer returns to the scene of his crime. Was he coming here to torture himself? Adam shook his head impatiently. "Don't be an ass," he told himself. "You're not a murderer. Don't be morbid. You're coming here to thank an old man for helping you."

Defiantly he walked down the road to Mr. Cohen's house. He found Mr. Cohen in old overalls at the back of his house turning over a small plot of land with a hoe. The old man put down the tool and gave him a warm welcome.

"Hello, young fellow, glad to see you. Out walking?"

"Well, yes. But I came to see you. I wanted to thank you for your help Saturday night. You were terrific. I don't know what I would have done without you."

Mr. Cohen made a gesture of dismissal. "I didn't do anything. How's the girl? Any news?"

Adam shook his head. "I haven't heard anything. I don't know."

Mr. Cohen gave him a keen look. "You're not very welcome up there, at the hospital I mean, are you?"

"Not by her brother. He's pretty mad. I can't blame him. He thinks it was my fault, and I suppose in a way it was. If we'd only gone back to get a helmet. . . . I had an old one at home. It might not have fit her, but it would have helped."

It was a relief to talk to someone. Harry had been busy with exams, so they had seen each other only briefly, and Adam had said he didn't want to talk about the accident yet. But now the words came pouring out. "It's awful, not being able to go up to see her. I know it doesn't matter. I mean, whether I see her or not isn't going to help her. It's all selfish. I shouldn't be thinking of myself at all or feeling sorry for myself. Here I am, not a scratch on me, and I don't even know if she's going to live. You don't know how terrible it is; no one knows. I feel so ashamed. . . ."

"I understand," Mr. Cohen said gently, "but you have nothing to be ashamed of. Who knows if a helmet would have made any difference? It was an accident. Don't beat yourself up, young man."

"I know. I'm sorry. I came here to thank you, and instead I'm pouring out my troubles. Say, I can turn up this dirt for you. You making a garden?"

"A little one. My wife likes fresh vegetables; they taste different when you pick them yourself."

Adam picked up the hoe and started to work. The earth was a rich, deep brown, and watching it turn over made him feel good. Mr. Cohen sat on a folding chair and watched him. "It would take me all afternoon," he said with an indulgent smile. "You do it in no time. It's good to be young."

"Sometimes," Adam said ruefully.

"Don't fool yourself. You're only young for a short while; enjoy it while you can. Take my word for it. This girl, Jenny, is she your girl?"

Adam leaned on the hoe handle for a few seconds before he answered. "That's hard to answer. I hardly know her—it was our first date—and yet I feel I've known her forever. I can't explain it. It sounds stupid, doesn't it?"

Mr. Cohen smiled. "Stupid, no. Human, yes. Sometimes I feel that way about my wife. Forty years of marriage, and there are times I feel I don't know her. Yet other times I feel I've known her much longer than forty years. It's not such a bad feeling."

When Adam finished digging the garden patch, he said good-bye to Mr. Cohen and left. He walked home glad that he had gone and hoped that he wouldn't lose too quickly the good feeling Mr. Cohen had given him.

When Adam did get home he felt so good he decided to develop the pictures of Jenny. Eagerly he got out the roll of film and went into his dark-room, a small room he had fixed up in a corner of the basement playroom.

Adam worked, whistling softly to himself, until he had a batch of contact prints. He examined each picture carefully and in a flurry of excitement se-lected three to make prints of. He knew it was time for dinner and that his mother would be calling him, but he couldn't wait. He went on working.

Sure enough, soon he could hear, "Adam, Adam, come to dinner."

"I'm busy," Adam yelled up the stairs. "You go ahead. I'll eat later."

It was after ten o'clock when Adam came upstairs, but he went directly to his room with his pictures. Behind his closed door and with his brightest light on, he stood the prints on his bureau against the wall. They were three pictures of Jenny on her skates: one, standing, laughing at him; another in motion, her body lean and graceful; and the third, in profile, taken as she turned around to glance at him with her dark, sparkling eyes. Sharply clear, all three of them caught her liveliness. Adam studied each, trying to pick one to blow up to give to Jenny. Fi-nally he decided to enlarge all three.

71

When Adam finally came down to the kitchen to eat, his mother came in to join him. "I'm glad you haven't given up your photography at least."

"Whatever made you think I would?"

"Just the way you've been acting lately. Have you some new pictures?"

"Some things I took a while ago," Adam said casually, helping himself to cold steak and salad.

"Can they be seen?"

"Nothing interesting," he said.

"All your photos interest me."

"These wouldn't." Adam busied himself with his food, aware of his mother's eyes, anxious and annoyed, on him. He got up from the table. "I'll take my plate upstairs. I've got some homework to do."

In his room, he took the pictures and put them in the bottom drawer of his dresser, underneath all the heavy winter sweaters, scarves, and woolen caps. "And she better not look for them either," he muttered to himself, banging the drawer shut with his foot. He was still feeling pretty good when he sat down to finish his supper and read a book.

5

On Wednesday, the fourth day after her date with
Adam DeWitt, Jenny Melino opened her eyes at
4:35 in the morning. She wanted to say something,
but no words came out. "Mom's sweater . . . it's
torn. . . ." She could say the words in her head,
but she heard only peculiar sounds coming from her
throat. Instinctively she tried to touch her neck, but
she found that she couldn't lift her hand. Her right

arm and hand were lying at her side; she could see them, but she couldn't move them. Her left arm was bandaged.

Studying her arm, Jenny suddenly realized that she was in a bed. Her eyes roamed around the room, and she panicked. It wasn't her room; it wasn't her bed. She lifted her left hand slowly to her face, and her fingers met tubes. One was coming out of her nose; there were bandages on her head, a bandage on her throat, a tube attached to her arm. She wanted to call for help, but her voice was only that frightening, hoarse whisper. She wanted to get up, but her body felt like a ton. Nothing worked. She felt as if she had been moved into another body that wouldn't do what she wanted. Jenny wondered if that had happened, or perhaps she was dreaming. . . .

"Hello, Jenny," said a soft voice, and then a face floated into view. A friendly face. A face with a smile.

"Help me, please. Get me out." They weren't real words, just queer noises.

"Sh-sh, don't try to talk. And don't look so frightened. You've been in an accident, and you're in the hospital, but you're going to be all right. The doctor will be here in a moment, and after that you can see your mother. Would you like that?"

74

"My mother's working; she's not here. I tore her sweater." It hurt Jenny to try to talk, but she had to explain. It was very important for this nurse with the white cap to understand. Jenny was pleased that she knew the lady was a nurse, and she wanted to tell her so, but the woman had disappeared.

Feeling tired, Jenny closed her eyes. When she opened them, the nurse was back and a man was with her. He was lifting Jenny's legs, first one and then the other.

"She was confused," the nurse was saying. "She wanted to talk. I could read her lips. She insisted her mother was working, and she was upset about tearing a sweater."

"She's disoriented, and no wonder," the man said. "I'm not worried about that. It'll clear up."

That nurse had it all wrong. She was the one who was confused, not Jenny. Jenny felt compelled to set them straight. "My mother is so working." She had meant to yell, but all she could manage was another hoarse whisper.

The nurse looked unhappy. "Poor little thing," she said, "she looks so scared." The nurse had a sharp pointed nose and a lot of brown freckles, and Jenny decided she looked like a terrier mutt they once had. She wished she'd go away. She didn't like her anymore. The man was nicer. He had gentle hands and pleasant blue eyes. He was examining her, so she supposed he must be a doctor. But she was too tired to think and drifted off to sleep again.

When Jenny awoke several hours later, her mother was sitting beside her. She tried to take hold of her mother's hand, but again she found she couldn't move her right arm. "Stupid arm won't move," Jenny mumbled. "Why aren't you working?"

"I'm taking time off to be with you. Don't worry about that." Her mother bent down and kissed her gently. "Sh-sh, you're not supposed to talk."

"My voice is funny. And my throat hurts."

"You had a little operation on your throat, but it will be better soon. Try to be quiet, darling."

"I tore your sweater."

"Don't worry about my sweater. I don't care about the sweater."

"I want to go home, Mom. Take me home."

"I wish I could, but you'll have to stay here for a while. Until you're better."

"I want to go home." Jenny began to whimper. She felt like a baby and sounded like one to her own ears. But she didn't care. She could feel the tears on her cheeks. "Please take me home." She made a move to get out of bed, but she was attached to too many tubes, and, besides, she couldn't move her right leg. It felt like a lump of wood.

When Jenny was told that she had been in the hospital in a coma for three days and three nights, she found the thought incomprehensible. What had happened in that time? How could she have not known anything, not felt anything for all that time? Not eaten, not dreamed, not talked . . . it was scary. She became afraid to go to sleep, afraid she might never wake up. She didn't tell anyone, but each night she was determined to stay awake. But sooner or later she drifted off to sleep in spite of her resolution.

During the following days the only way Jenny could mark time was by the tests she received. Yesterday she'd had a second brain scan. The doctor had explained patiently what he was going to do, but she had only half listened. She had been just as scared the second time as the first. The nurses had looked too anxious. She was learning to tell by the expressions on their faces whether they were going to do something painful or dangerous.

But maybe she hadn't had the second brain scan

yesterday. Maybe it had been the EEG or the angiogram. But then what day was it they had done the spinal tap? It was all too confusing. She wasn't allowed to get up even to go to the bathroom; her body hurt all the time. The nurse promised that she would get out of intensive care soon, very soon. But when? "Then we'll get you up and dressed, and you'll be able to go into the solarium and watch television." The nurse spoke as cheerily as if that was the greatest treat she could imagine.

"Good morning, Jenny. How are you today?" The bearded Dr. Fine had just arrived. As usual, he had a group of young doctors with him.

"I'm fine." They had plugged up the hole in her throat so she could speak a little better. The tube still remained, but its removal was another promise.

"That's good. What's your name?"

"Jenny Melino." He always asked her the same foolish questions.

"What day of the week is it?"

"I don't know. I've been trying to figure that out."

"You came in last Saturday night. You slept until Wednesday. You've been awake for three days. So what day is it?"

Jenny counted out loud. "Wednesday, Thursday, Friday. Today's Saturday?"

"That's right. Good girl. And who was the first president of the United States?"

"George Washington."

"Right." Dr. Fine turned to his colleagues. "You see, she's alert enough." He spoke as proudly as if he had given the answers. Then he thumped her body in various places and manipulated her arms and legs. "Do you feel that?" He gave her right leg a hard whack.

Jenny shook her head. "No, I don't feel anything." Nothing on her right side seemed to be in working order, and she still couldn't move her right arm or leg. Dr. Fine spoke to the doctors grouped around him, using medical terms Jenny didn't understand.

"What's the matter with me anyway?" Jenny asked. "Why can't I get out of bed?"

"I hope you will soon," Dr. Fine said. "You gave yourself a pretty hard bump on the head, and we want to make sure we know exactly where you hurt yourself." He sounded jovial.

"Can't I even go to the bathroom?"

"I'm afraid if you got up you'd find you couldn't walk. You see, your brain controls every move you make. To put it simply, one area of your brain controls what you can do with certain parts of your

79

body. From all the X rays and tests it looks as if you hit certain spots in your brain hard enough to prevent their sending the proper signals to the right side of your body. That's why you can't move your leg or arm. Until the lesions heal, you won't do much walking."

Jenny's stomach turned over. "What if they don't heal?"

"We hope they will. Your chances are good if you help, but you're going to have to work hard. We'll talk about it later." Dr. Fine turned away abruptly, and his group followed him to the next patient.

Jenny began to cry softly. Those doctors unnerved her. They examined her as if she were a laboratory specimen rather than a person. And they wouldn't tell her anything. They made comments in complicated medical terms that she didn't understand but that frightened her.

She was crying when her mother came in. "Jenny, darling, what's the matter? Are you in pain? What happened?"

"I can't walk. Maybe I'll never walk again. Mommy. . . ." Jenny grabbed her mother's hand with her good one and held it fast. "Do you think I'll be a cripple?"

"Who said you would be a cripple? It's not true,

80

darling. I know it's not true. Who told you that?"

A nurse appeared at the bedside. It was Miss Rodriguez, the pretty Puerto Rican one. "You can only stay a few minutes," she said kindly to Mrs. Melino. "What's the matter with Jenny?"

"Someone told her she wouldn't walk again. Whoever said such a thing?" Mrs. Melino was trying to control her own fright.

"Dr. Fine said so." Jenny sobbed. "He said something happened to my head so I couldn't walk. . . ."

"He meant just temporarily." Miss Rodriguez stuck a thermometer in her mouth. "It will take time for everything to heal. Then you'll be fine. But you're going to have to help, and crying is no good. Anyway, I've got good news for you. You're going to get something to eat. Real soup. Would you like that? I'm going to take this tube out."

Miss Rodriguez took out the thermometer and proceeded to disconnect the intravenous feeding apparatus, an act that seemed to give her more satisfaction than it did Jenny. "Sorry, Mrs. Melino, but you'll have to go." She ushered her out, barely giving her a chance to kiss Jenny good-bye.

Alone, Jenny wriggled her body and moved her good leg, just to prove to herself that she could. Miserably she watched a blue robe her mother had brought slide off the bed to the floor. She could see the splash of bright blue, and she decided she wanted to get it. Why not? she thought. I'll find out if I can walk.

Free of the IV, Jenny threw her good leg over the side of the bed and pulled herself up to a sitting position. Slowly she maneuvered herself to the bed's edge until she could touch the floor with her foot. Then with her left hand she lifted her right leg and put it over the side to dangle alongside her other leg. Slowly and painfully Jenny pulled herself upright and stood, putting her weight on her left foot. She stood that way for a few seconds. Hanging on to the table beside the bed, she took a step forward on her left foot and tried to drag her right leg along. But she didn't have the strength. Instead, she fell, crashing headlong to the floor alongside her bed. She heard the noise of glass breaking—probably something on the table—quick footsteps, Miss Rodriguez's voice shrieking, "Jenny!" and then she blacked out.

6

Jenny wasn't out for long. As she was being lifted back into bed she could hear the sound of Miss Rodriguez's heavily accented voice. "What did you think you were doing? You foolish child. Imagine getting out of bed! *Dios mio.* . . ."

"I thought I could walk." Jenny moaned. "It looked so easy. I just wanted to pick up my bathrobe."

"Easy, my, my. . . . You have to be patient." Miss Rodriguez plumped up her pillow and smoothed her sheets. "Be patient, my child."

Be patient. That's what everyone said. The doctors, the nurses, her mother. She was trying, but it was so boring. And everything hurt so much. Just to lift her bandaged arm to scratch her nose was an ordeal. There wasn't even any television to watch until she got out of Intensive Care. (At least, she had learned that the initials ICU meant Intensive Care Unit.) "When will I get out of here?" Jenny asked.

"You were supposed to be moved today, but I don't know now with your climbing out of bed. I don't know how you got as far as you did so fast. I just went over to check Mrs. Epstein; my back was turned for less than a minute." Miss Rodriguez was very upset. "You could have hurt yourself seriously."

Jenny didn't say that her good leg and arm hurt and that her head was throbbing. Maybe if she didn't tell them anything, she'd get out sooner. "You could get me into trouble, too," Miss Rodriguez continued. "How do you think I'm going to explain your getting out of bed?"

"No one has to know," Jenny said.

"A lot you know about it. Everything goes down

84

on your chart, young lady. Every single thing. What you eat and what you get rid of. No secrets in a hospital, my dear."

Jenny was only half listening. She wanted to close her eyes and think about nice things . . . food, roller skating, or Adam. . . .

She drifted off to sleep. When she woke up, her mother was there with a nurse, an attendant, and a wheelchair. Jenny's eyes fastened on the wheelchair. "What's that for?"

"That's for you, my dear," the nurse said cheerfully. "You're going to be moved. Aren't you glad?"

"Am I going home?" Jenny asked eagerly.

"No, darling," her mother answered. "Not yet. But you're going to a more cheerful room."

The attendant picked Jenny up in his arms and deposited her in the wheelchair. "Are you comfortable?" the nurse asked.

Jenny stared down and mumbled a response.

"What's the matter?"

"Do I have to go to another room? Can't I go home?"

"Jenny, darling, you want to get well, don't you?" Mrs. Melino tucked the blue robe around her. "You're going to start getting physical therapy to help you. You can't have that at home."

"Why hasn't Adam come to see me?" Jenny asked her mother as the attendant pushed her down the hall and into an elevator.

"No one was allowed to come except Mike and me. Do you want to see Adam?" Her mother's voice was hesitant.

"Why shouldn't I? Isn't he okay? You said he was."

"He's fine. I just thought . . . I don't know. Mike is very angry about Adam. It may not be such a good idea."

"I don't care what Mike thinks. He didn't like Adam before. You could let Adam know that he can come now, couldn't you? I mean, if he wants to."

"I'll be diplomatic. Don't worry."

Jenny was wheeled into a room that held four beds. Two were occupied, one by a gray-haired woman, the other by a woman who appeared to be in her twenties. Jenny was taken to the empty bed by the window, which pleased her. She wouldn't have admitted it to a soul, but she was glad to get back into bed. Her whole body had ached while she'd been sitting in the wheelchair.

Inadvertently she let out a sigh as she settled against the pillows. "You're glad to be back in bed," the nurse said.

Jenny shrugged. The nurse laughed. "Stubborn, aren't you? You won't admit it. You haven't seen the bruises all over your body. You don't have to tell me they hurt when you move around. They want you to start therapy, but I don't know. . . ."

"I guess the doctor thinks it's all right," Louise interjected.

Jenny didn't feel like talking, and she was relieved when her mother said she had some errands to do and would come back later. As she looked out the window she thought longingly of her room at home. It wasn't much of a room. It had only a single window—a dormer facing west—which made it beastly hot in the summer. So to get any air she had to leave the door open. But at least it was private.

Privacy was important to Jenny. She liked to be able to go up to her room, close the door, and be alone. Often her mother asked, "What on earth do you do up there by yourself?" Jenny was never able to tell her. She didn't do much. Sometimes she did nothing at all; she just lay across her bed so she could see the sky and listened to her transistor radio. Sometimes she read books she took from the library or looked at magazines her mother brought home. Or she'd fiddle with her hair and fix it in different ways. A good part of the time she spent thinking about things and people, the girls in school, the clothes and records she'd buy if she had the money.

Going out with Adam had seemed a small window to the world she thought about. Not because he was rich, but because he had what she called "class." He represented a contact with another life, far removed from East Street. And he wasn't standoffish and condescending like the girls in school. He had acted as if he really liked her, ordinary Jenny Melino whose mother worked in a bar.

But going out with Adam had turned into a disaster. Now, lying in bed, Jenny began to wonder about what had been in Adam's mind. Had he really liked her, or had he something else in mind . . . ?

Jenny dozed off to sleep. When she awoke, it was late afternoon and Adam was standing beside her bed. Jenny was so surprised she didn't know what to say. She hadn't thought he'd come so soon.

"Hello." Adam gave her a soft smile. "How're you doing?"

"I'm good."

"Are you really? I mean, are you really okay?"

Jenny laughed to cover her confusion. "I don't know. They don't really know what's the matter with me yet. There's a chair over there if you want to sit down."

Adam pulled the chair close to the bed. "I didn't know if you wanted to see me. I thought you might be mad. . . ."

"Why should I be mad?"

"Your brother thinks the accident was my fault."

Jenny stared silently at her feet sticking up under the thin blanket. "Was it?" she asked quietly, and looked up at him.

Adam held her eyes solemnly. "I don't think so. I could kill myself for not having gone back for the helmet, but I don't see how anyone can say the accident was my fault. It was a set of miserable circumstances—the bump, your getting something in your eye. I keep going over the whole thing in my mind until I feel as if I'm going nuts. Maybe it *was* my fault. Do you think it was?"

"I don't know." Jenny gave a deep sigh. "It doesn't really matter, does it? I mean, blaming you isn't going to help me." She felt unreasonably irritated by his concern about whose fault it was. As if that mattered now.

"It's important to me. I can hardly think of anything else. It's hard to explain."

"What is?" Jenny felt tired, but she tried to pay attention.

Adam looked embarrassed. "This is going to sound

crazy to you, but I've got to tell you. I love you. Don't look at me like that. It's the truth. Honest to God. I think about you all the time."

Jenny stared at him. What was he talking about?

Adam took her hand. "I do love you; it has nothing to do with what's happened."

Jenny's face flushed with anger. How dare he hand her such a line! "You must think I'm pretty dumb. I don't need you to feel sorry for me." She couldn't find the words to express her fury and humiliation. "You love me. That's a laugh. You don't even know me. I've been thinking too. What'd you take me on that lake road for, anyway? Why'd you suddenly want to date Jenny Melino? The girls you know wouldn't come across, and you thought I would? Mike is right; you are a punk. Now you say you love me! That is too much."

Adam stood listening, his face flaming. "That's stupid. I don't blame you for being mad at me, at the whole world, but if you think I'm just feeling sorry for you, you're dead wrong. I asked you out because I thought you were real, not a phony like a lot of other girls, but maybe I was wrong. Maybe you're dumb enough to believe what your great brother tells you!" Adam turned and walked out of the room.

Jenny watched the door close behind him. Everything had happened so fast. She couldn't believe it. She wanted to run after him, to call him back; she didn't want him to leave her this way. It was too cruel for him to walk out on her. But she had been mean too; she didn't know which of them had been more hurtful.

Oh, God, to be so helpless. She had wanted so much to see Adam. Why had she exploded like that? Why?

7

Adam was furious with himself. He had gone to visit Jenny with such hope, had wanted so desperately to see her, and he had blown it completely. Though all their meetings seemed to turn into disaster, Adam refused to give up. The situation was enough to make him think Mike had put a hex on them, but that was stupid.

A few days after his visit to Jenny, Adam went

out for a walk. The moon was up, but there was a wind coming in from the north, and Adam thought that a summer northeaster might be on its way. It was the kind of night he liked, one that held the existing promise of a storm about to break.

Without any prior destination, Adam headed toward the village. After crossing the railroad tracks, he found himself on Railroad Street. The thought came to him that there was no reason why he couldn't stop at the bar and ask Mrs. Melino about Jenny. The few times they had met she had been cordial, and he didn't think she would mind.

Adam was just about to enter the bar when he saw Mike standing inside. At that moment Mike looked up and saw him too; it was too late to turn back.

The room was empty except for one old man sitting at a table sipping a beer. Mike was behind the bar; Mrs. Melino was not in sight. Adam stood near the door and said, "I came to see your mother, but I guess she's not here."

"She'll be right back," Mike said gruffly. "What d'you want to see her about?"

"I'll come back another time." Adam put his hand on the door and started to leave.

"What's the matter? You scared? Maybe you're

right. Railroad Street's a dangerous place, full of Wops and Polacks."

"Why don't you give up?" Adam turned to face Mike. Mike came out from behind the bar and took hold of Adam's shoulder.

"Listen, you," Mike said, "I hear you went to see my sister. If you know what's good for you, you won't do that again. You just take yourself off to your Harvard like a good little boy, do your homework, and leave Jenny Melino alone. You hear?"

Adam tried to get out of Mike's grasp, but his hold was firm. "Take your hands off me! Harvard sure seems to bother you, doesn't it? That chip on your shoulder must weigh a ton. What's the matter? Has the world given you a bum deal? Does everyone else have the brains and the luck? Poor Mike." Adam finally pulled away. His sarcasm was making Mike furious. "Get wise to yourself. Did it ever occur to you that I *am* smarter than you are? You're not going to tell me what to do or who to see. Understand?"

"You smart? You make me laugh. Without your father's money you couldn't get a job as a ditch-digger. You can't even ride a motorcycle without half killing someone. And you're chicken, besides. Fighting you would be like fighting a marsh-mallow."

"You want to try?" Adam started to take off his jacket.

Mike glanced at the old man and at the empty bar. "You'll be slaughtered. . . ."

"Come on outside," Adam said tersely.

In a minute the boys were grappling on the ground. Mike was stronger, but Adam was quicker. Both boys were hitting hard.

"Stop this! Stop, both of you. Stop this minute. . . ." Louise Melino was standing over them, yelling. She got hold of Mike's shirt and pulled. "You stop!" The shirt ripped, and Adam and Mike fell apart. "Are you two crazy? Haven't we got enough trouble without you making fools of yourselves? Oh, God. Go inside, Mike, and wash your face. You go home," she said, turning to Adam, while Mike stood glowering.

"I'm sorry." Adam wiped his face with his shirt-tail and picked up his jacket from where he had dropped it.

"I don't know what started this, but I can imagine." Mrs. Melino put her hand on Mike's arm. "Come on." She pushed him to the door, and they both went into the bar.

Adam turned and slowly walked toward home. He wasn't sorry they had fought. Now he knew why

Mike hated him so, and it wasn't only because of the accident. Mike was a jackass, but he had unwittingly crystallized a problem that had been disturbing Adam: Did he really want to go to Harvard?

Harvard was taken for granted in the DeWitt family. Adam's father was a Harvard man, and so were his brothers, Adam's two uncles. Adam had assumed he would follow in their footsteps, but now things looked different. If a sudden accident could change Jenny's life so completely, the same thing could happen to him. The thought was frightening, and it made him want to keep control of his life whenever he could. Just drifting along now, going to Harvard before he was sure of what he wanted, was letting his parents stay in control. Do your homework like a good little boy . . . obey the grown-ups . . . grow up to be a lawyer like Daddy. . . . In his crude way Mike had put his finger on it. It was their plan, their way of life; Adam wanted to be very sure it was his, too.

On his way home he decided he would not go to Harvard in the fall. Maybe next year, maybe not. He'd have to give it a lot of thought. Wouldn't Mike gloat if he knew he had been an influence? The irony tickled Adam. He probably would have made the same decision eventually, but Mike had helped him to see the issues involved.

Now Adam had to face telling his parents, and he decided the quicker that was done the better.

When Adam got home, his parents were sitting on the patio, talking. Judging by the abrupt silence that fell as he approached, Adam sensed that he had been the topic of conversation. He cleared his throat. "There's something I'd like to tell you both," he said, somewhat stiffly.

"Yes?" Adam thought his father seemed hostile. His mother looked alarmed.

"I've been thinking about this a lot," Adam said untruthfully, "and I've decided I want to hold off going to college for a year. It really makes sense," he continued hurriedly, not wanting to give his father a chance to speak. "There are a lot of things I have to think about, and I want to be sure that when I go to Harvard I'm ready to get the most out of it. No sense wasting your good money," he added, with a laugh.

"Since when have you started to worry about wasting my money?" Mr. DeWitt asked. "I don't know how much thought you've given this ridiculous decision—and I doubt it's a lot—but you're moving in the wrong direction. The sooner you get away from here the better, and I consider it fortunate for all of us that you are scheduled to leave for Cambridge in the fall. I only wish it was sooner. So get any ideas about staying home out of your head."

"Sorry, Dad, but I've made up my mind. I don't think you can talk me out of it. I know Harvard's a sacred word around this house, and I know everything you're going to say. How lucky I am to get in, what a privilege it is. But I'm going to have to make up my own mind."

His mother had been looking at him closely. "What happened to your lip? It's bleeding. And you're so dirty. Where have you been?"

"I was out walking."

"You look as if you've been rolling in the mud," she said.

"More likely you've been in a fight," his father said. "Were you?"

"I'm okay."

"Who were you fighting with?" his father demanded.

"Some kid. You don't know him."

"What about?"

"Hey, you cross-examining me? It was just a scuffle, not important."

"It had to do with that girl. I can tell by your face," his mother said, eyeing him sharply. "I agree with your father. You need to get away from here."

"You're both wrong. The accident has little to do with my decision," Adam said, less than frankly, "but if I were looking for another reason to stay here, that would be one. I'm not running away."

Suddenly Adam felt very tired. He turned and left the patio, heading upstairs. His room was dark, and instead of turning on any light, he went over to a window and knelt on the floor, resting his arms on the sill. He could see the lamps in other houses, and the string of lights along the highway; in the distance were a few lights he knew to belong to cottages on a finger of the lake. He thought about Mr. and Mrs. Cohen and wondered if they had any children—probably grandchildren by now. They had looked old to him. But he felt that Mr. Cohen would understand why he didn't want to go away. He had been unusually gentle and sympathetic the night of the accident, even coming to the hospital when there had been no real need.

And Jenny? Adam wondered what Jenny would

think. She probably wouldn't care one way or another. But maybe she would. She might be disappointed. He remembered how pleased she had looked when she congratulated him. She had liked going out with someone who was going to Harvard. A lot of good it had done her!

Don't think about Jenny, Adam told himself, as he turned on a lamp and picked up a book he had been reading. But the story no longer interested him. He stretched out on his bed and stared up at the ceiling, and after a while he closed his eyes and fell asleep. Sometime after midnight thunder woke him up, and he threw off his clothes and crawled under the covers. To the comforting sound of rain on the roof he fell back into a deep sleep.

8

"The kids at school miss you," Kate said. She was sitting on Jenny's bed while Jenny sat in the wheelchair.

"Yeah?" Jenny's eyes were on the door. One of the nurses had promised to bring her some juice; she was dying of thirst. "They gave us salty ham for lunch today." She brought her attention back to Kate. "What's new? What's going on?"

"Not much. We had a stinky algebra exam, and Mrs. Dennis was out sick. The substitute was awful. Candy's going to have a party for her birthday next week. I can't decide what to get for her. What do you think? Maybe a box of pretty writing paper would be nice. She's always writing to that boy she met last summer. You think she'd like that?" Kate looked at Jenny for an answer, but Jenny's eyes were closed. "You tired? You falling asleep?"

"No. It's just. . . . Darn, I wish she'd come with something to drink."

"Should I get you some water?"

"No, the water tastes funny."

"Do you think writing paper would be good?"

"Writing paper? Good for what?"

"What's the matter with you? You weren't listening at all."

"I'm sorry." Jenny was sorry, but school and all the other things Kate was concerned about—the things she herself used to be interested in—now seemed so remote from her present life.

"The kids all want to know when you're coming out of here," Kate said.

"I don't know. They're moving me to a rehab place."

"What's that?"

"Rehabilitation."

Kate giggled. "Sounds like something for old folks."

"This one's for children. They're supposed to teach me how to get along."

"Get along?"

Jenny looked at her squarely. "If I can't walk. Or if I have only one good arm. They teach you how to do things, to eat and get dressed and stuff like that."

Kate looked frightened. "Your mother said not to talk about it."

Jenny's face was grim. "Why shouldn't I talk about it? They think I'm stupid. I know they don't know if I'm ever going to be okay. They say the rehab place is to help me, but nobody knows. The doctor himself told me he doesn't know. He can't promise anything; they can do more therapy in the rehab place, that's all. Maybe it'll work and maybe it won't."

"It will," Kate said. "I'm sure it will."

Jenny gave a harsh laugh. "You know. You know more than the doctors?"

"I know you. You'll make it work," Kate said, with bright eyes.

Jenny was excited about riding in the ambulance,

but nervous about moving to Hilltop House, the rehabilitation center. "Did you bring Suky?" she asked her mother. Suky was a hand-crotcheted, floppy-eared dog, made by a friend of Mrs. Melino's, that decorated Jenny's room at home.

"Yes, I brought Suky. And the books you asked for, and a new blouse and skirt."

"What do I need them for?"

"Because at Hilltop you get dressed every day. No one sits around in a bathrobe. I brought some of your other clothes, too."

"What if I want to be in my bathrobe?"

Mrs. Melino had been gathering Jenny's toilet articles into a shopping bag. She put the bag down and looked at Jenny steadily. "Listen, Jenny." She spoke in a quiet, even voice. "I know you're having one hell of a time, and I would give everything I've got, including my own life, to undo this for you. But, *please*, don't start off at Hilltop antagonizing everyone. They're there to help you, but you've got to help yourself."

Jenny lowered her eyes. She didn't answer her mother. Instead she said, "What time is the ambulance supposed to come?"

Mrs. Melino consulted her watch. "In about half

an hour, I'm going to call a nurse to help dress you."

The trip didn't take more than three-quarters of an hour. All that Jenny could see as she approached Hilltop was a glimpse of rolling lawns and tall shade trees. She couldn't see much of the sprawling stone building either, but it didn't seem too depressing. "Lots of grass and flower borders," her mother remarked.

"What good is that going to do me?" Jenny asked.

Jenny's stretcher was wheeled into a wide corridor, and while her mother stopped at the admission office Jenny saw some children in wheelchairs zooming down the hall at breakneck speed. One girl, stretched out flat on her stomach was going equally fast on a self-propelled stretcher. Jenny shuddered, thinking, They must be crazy to go that fast.

In a few minutes a tall, handsome, black woman, smartly dressed in a sweater and denim skirt, came out of an office and greeted Jenny. "Hello, Jenny," she said. "Welcome to Hilltop. I'm Sally Flanner, your social worker. I'm kind of your special advisor. The medical staff sets up your program, but I'll help you get into activities, and anytime you have a problem just holler. I'll try to help. I can't always, but

I'll try. I hope you'll like it here; I think you will."

"Maybe, but I doubt it."

Sally Flanner laughed. "Well, you're honest anyway. Good. I am too. After you get settled in your room, I'll come and we can talk about it. See you later." She turned and left a somewhat surprised Jenny.

Sally Flanner reappeared when Jenny was settled in her bed and her mother was putting away her clothes. She introduced herself to Mrs. Melino. "You can call me Sally," she said to them both. "It's easier to remember than Flanner."

Sally pulled up a chair next to Jenny's bed. "So you don't expect to like it here. Can you tell me why? I mean, besides being mad that you had an accident and won't be having a good time this summer. Anyone would get mad about that."

"Then I guess I'm like everyone else," Jenny mumbled.

"Yes and no. Some kids have the sense to want to get well. All kinds come here. Some are a pain in the neck and some try to help. It's up to you to decide which you want to be."

"But it's all a waste of time."

"What do you mean?"

106

"Nobody thinks I'm going to walk again, so what's the use of going through all this? It's dumb."

"Where did you get the idea you were never going to walk again?" Sally asked her candidly.

"Nobody said I would. The doctors said they didn't know."

"That's true. They don't know. But that doesn't mean you won't." She shrugged. "It's up to you. I happen to think that if you work at it, really work on your exercising, you're going to be fine. I've seen it happen with others."

After Sally and her mother left, Jenny turned her face into her pillow. She was afraid. She felt alone. Everything here was new and strange, and she didn't know anyone. She was miles from home; her friends wouldn't even know where to find her.

Jenny's panic grew as she heard children's voices and the noise of wheelchairs going down the hall. She was afraid of all those brave, heroic children Sally described—the ones who never complained about their handicaps and their diseases. She didn't want to be a heroine. She wanted to be just plain Jenny Melino, who could jump and run and roller-skate and *walk*.

Her door flew open with a crash, and one of the roller beds came zooming into the room. A young girl, lying on her stomach, was on it, her body encased in a heavy cast that started somewhere above her knees and went up around part of her neck. A loose gown was draped over it. Her head lifted to look at Jenny. "Hi, I'm Helene, Helene Fitzpatrick, your roommate. You can call me Lanie. Everyone does. What's your name?"

"Jenny. Jenny Melino. Hello." Jenny stared at the girl's face. She was beautiful. A mop of dark hair piled on top of her head framed a delicate, pale face with wide-set violet eyes and a straight, aristocratic nose. It was a lively face, with a mouth quick to smile. It didn't belong with a body in a heavy cast. Somehow Jenny had never imagined that any of the kids at Hilltop would be attractive. She had thought they'd all look peculiar.

"What's the matter?" Lanie asked. "Why're you staring at me? Didn't you ever see anyone in a body cast before?"

"I wasn't staring at that," Jenny said, embarrassed. "You get around well in that thing, don't you?" She watched Lanie maneuver herself over to her bureau and pick up a brush. Lanie shook her head until the hair fell down around her face, and then she began to brush it.

"I should. I've been in it long enough. What's the matter with you?"

Jenny told her about the motorcycle accident. "And you?"

"I've got something called 'scoliosis.' In plain English it's curvature of the spine. I was operated on and had a rod in my back for months before this cast. It's supposed to be all right when they take it off. I hope so." She seemed very casual.

"Don't you care?" Jenny asked. "I mean, don't you mind being in that thing?"

Lanie stared at her and then laughed. "Are you kidding? Of course I mind. But if I wasn't operated on, I'd probably never be able to stand up straight. This is only a year out of my life; it's worth it."

"At least, you know you're going to be all right. My situation is different."

Lanie put her brush down to look at Jenny. "Everyone here is different, but we're all alike too. We've all got something stupid the matter with us, something we didn't ask for. You coming down for supper? You can ring for someone to get you out of bed."

"I'm staying here. I don't feel like going any-where. I guess I'm tired from the trip."

Lanie smiled. "You're homesick. Everyone's home-sick in the beginning. I cried like crazy the whole first night I was here. But it's not so bad. You'll get used to it. They keep you so busy there's not much time to be lonesome, except at night."

Jenny listened to Lanie's roller bed racing down the hall and to the noise of other children going to the dining hall. She was glad she had asked to eat in her room. She didn't want to meet those children; she didn't want to see their crutches or their wheel-chairs or face their staring eyes. All she wanted was to get out of this place as fast as she could.

9

Adam had Jenny's pictures propped up on his bureau against the wall. He and Harry were looking at them. "She's beautiful, isn't she?" Adam said from the floor, where he was leaning against a bright-orange hassock.

"Yeah, she's good-looking."

"What's the matter? You don't think so?"

111

"I think you should forget about her."

"Christ, you sound like my mother. All right, let's talk about Israel. What do you suggest doing about the Palestinian refugees?"

"I could introduce you to a nice Jewish girl. Would you like that?"

"That would really put my mother in a spot. She'd have to choose between Italian Jenny and Jewish Sayde."

"Sharon."

"Of course." Adam threw a rolled-up ball of paper at Harry. A few minutes later the boys were wrestling on the floor, laughing. Harry had Adam in a tight grip when Adam said, "Enough." Harry let go, and both boys stood up.

"Feel better?" Harry brushed dust from his clothes.

"Your psychiatry?"

"No, I have something better."

"Yeah?"

"Let's go down to the city tomorrow. There's supposed to be a terrific photography show at the Museum of Modern Art."

Adam laughed. "Mother's little helper. Okay, I don't mind."

"I'll pick you up at nine. We can make the nine twenty. And," Harry said at the door, "bring your camera along."

"Ha, ha, ha." Adam gave a mock laugh.

Alone, Adam stood looking at the pictures of Jenny for a long while before he carefully put them back in their hiding place.

Even though the boys got into New York City early on Saturday, the museum was already jammed. In spite of the crowd, Adam managed to get them both close enough to examine the photographs carefully. "For a well-brought-up youngster, you're not shy in a crowd," Harry remarked.

"You've got to be pushy in this world. I understand that's the only way to get ahead."

"Don't ask me."

"This man really gets detail, doesn't he?" Adam was examining a black-and-white landscape in which every blade of grass seemed to be distinct.

"He does it with a little machine."

"But it's not art. I know." Adam laughed. "He keeps his eyes closed and goes *click, click.*"

"Naturally. Say, look at this one. It looks like an etching."

"Which is art, he said enviously." Adam led Harry through the crowd, stopping to study a picture occasionally, not letting anyone hurry him.

They were near the main entrance again when Adam saw a young girl being helped into a museum wheelchair. While both her legs were in braces, she looked healthy and pretty from the waist up. "Come on, let's go," Harry said, following Adam's glance.

Adam stood still. "I wish I could talk to her."

"You can't."

"I know."

"Come on." Harry practically pushed him out the door onto 53rd Street. The day had become hot and sticky.

"Can you even imagine what it's like not to be able to walk? To be healthy in every way, but not to walk?" Adam looked down at their legs. "We take it so for granted."

"Thinking gets you nowhere."

"Exactly where I want to go."

"I'd prefer an Italian restaurant. Matter of fact, I know one. Follow me, lad." Harry turned around to walk west. Adam walked silently alongside him.

The restaurant was air-conditioned, the tables covered with red-checked cloths, and the spaghetti excellent. "Good living," Harry remarked.

"If you like that sort of thing. Living, I mean."

"After a while it comes naturally. You don't give it a thought. Seriously, isn't your breast beginning to hurt from all the beating? Enough's enough."

"Oh, I can go on for a long time. When I do something I do it thoroughly: accidents, breast-beating. . . . Did I ever tell you about Jenny's brother Mike?"

"Yes, you've told me about Jenny's brother Mike. A stocky, sinister fellow one should not meet in a dark alley. I'd know him anywhere."

"It is possible, just barely possible, that my deciding not to go to Harvard has a little bit to do with him. Hard to believe, wouldn't you say?"

"I'd say you'd lost that brilliant, sharp, logical mind of yours. Pity, too."

"Are you interested in knowing why?"

"Can't wait."

"Because I want the son of a bitch's approval. There it is, neat."

"Not at all. Full of holes. His approval? For what?"

"I don't know. I need to find out a lot of things, and that's one of them. I'm beginning to have a glimmer."

"So? Tell me."

"Because he's full of stupid prejudices against people who have more money than he. We're spoiled, we're selfish, we don't care—every cliché you can think of. I guess I want to show him that he's full of baloney. I want him to see me as a person, not as a member of a class. Get it?"

"Yeah, but why? Why do you care about teaching Mike Melino a lesson in sociology?"

"Because I'm everything he says I am, naturally. I'm a punk, self-centered, vain, spoiled. I can't stand that toad putting me down."

"If you like building walls around yourself, I know where there are a lot of bricks. Spumoni?"

"Yeah, sure. Let's go down to Little Italy and Chinatown, and I'll take some pictures."

"Now you're talking."

The boys took the subway downtown and walked along Mulberry Street. Adam didn't need much prodding to use his camera. "I could stay here for weeks taking pictures," he said, after shooting faces on the street, shopwindows hung with strings of garlic, cheeses, and sausages, old buildings. . . . "everywhere you look there's something."

From Little Italy they wandered over to Chinatown where the people and the colorful window displays were equally inviting to Adam. He used up two rolls of film before Harry said, smiling, "Enough? I think we'd better go if we want to make our train home."

"Yeah." Adam glanced at him. "Stop looking so smug. The big psychiatrist. You succeeded in getting the poor, sick boy out of himself. Now he can forget all his troubles and go to Harvard the way he's supposed to. Hurrah! I wrote that script when I was six years old."

"Too bad you didn't remember it."

"But I did. That's why I tore it up when I was twelve. It stinks."

"Sure, it stinks. Because your hero's a jerk. Mine isn't."

Riding in the subway back to Grand Central Station, Adam was quiet. He was still quiet when they got on the train.

"Okay," Harry said. "You trying to prove I failed?"

"Then you admit you were scheming?"

"My cunning Hebraic brain."

"Or my mother's Christian arrogance."

"Uh-uh. No one put me up to anything. Besides, I wanted to see the show at the museum."

"Okay, you tried. But it didn't work, at least not the way you expected it to. I'm not a complete fool;

I know this is going to fade after a while. If I have a kid someday, I'll tell him I'd rather he didn't get a motorcycle and probably won't even say why. Maybe by that time I won't remember Jenny's name. . . ." Adam laughed. "I doubt that. But I'll get over this, of course, I will. *But she won't.* Can you understand that? There is a very good chance she will be crippled for life. You'll have to admit that the realization is not the happiest thought to live with."

"If you insist on living with it. That's where we part company."

"We go around in circles. Sooner or later my living with it will fade. Okay, I agree to that. But in the meantime, for Christ's sake, let me suffer happily. Today was fine. I can even say I enjoyed myself. But the damn thing is, I'm not ready to shake off my depression yet. As a friend, I beg you, don't try to cheer me up. Okay?"

"Okay. Pinch me if I make a joke, God forbid."

"I'll break your bloody arm."

When they arrived at their station, Harry picked up the local weekly newspaper. "Here's something for you," he said to Adam, glancing through it. "A photo exhibit at the art center. Prizes, too. Next weekend. Entries accepted through Thursday. What will you submit?"

"If I enter."

"You can win a home computer. Add up all your debts."

"Thanks. I'll see. Maybe."

Harry gave him a sharp look. "I know one picture that would win in a minute."

"I do too." Adam knew they were both thinking of Jenny. "I'll think about it," was all he said.

10

The first week at Hilltop had gone quickly for Jenny, although, as she explained to Lanie, "Sometimes I feel that I've been here for years. I forget what it's like to do anything except go to therapy appointments, do exercises in the pool, go to this crazy school, and take more X rays and tests. What did we do before?"

"Plenty. But come on, we'll be late for supper."

Lanie was ready to wheel herself out of their room.

Jenny sat in her wheelchair. She had been taught how to move herself from her bed to her chair and back. "My big accomplishment," she had said bitterly. Jenny didn't hide her contempt for learning to adapt to her paralysis. "I don't want to learn how to be a cripple," she had yelled. "I want to learn how to walk."

"That will come later," she had been told. Maybe, Jenny thought to herself.

"Come on," Lanie repeated. "Let's go."

"I don't feel like eating. I despise that dining room."

"It's not the Plaza, but you've got to eat."

"The Plaza. I've heard about it, Mommy. Someday will you take me there?"

"If you're a good girl and eat up all your mush."

"Mush is right. You'd think once in a while they'd give us a steak."

"Dream on."

Reluctantly Jenny followed Lanie on her gurney, as they called the roller bed, to the dining room. She stopped at the doorway and groaned. "Oh, my God, are they out of their minds? Spaghetti! Even for healthy people it's hard to eat."

Jenny looked at the roomful of children, most of

them young, some of them spastic, many unable to hold a fork or spoon properly, trying to stuff strands of dripping spaghetti into their gaping mouths. Spaghetti was on their chins, in their laps, on the floor.

"They love it," Lanie said, but her face looked uneasy.

"I don't. I don't think I can take it."

"Just eat. Don't look."

"Yuck." Jenny knew that she couldn't turn around now, so she wheeled herself over to the farthest corner table. Lanie was transferred to a special chair, and Jenny was brought a plate of spaghetti on a tray that fitted over the arms of her wheelchair. She stared at the dish of food. "I can't begin to eat this," she said. "I can't do it with my left hand. I just can't."

"Well, you're going to try," a cheerful voice said.

Jenny looked up and saw Donna, a therapist she liked. "I've been looking for you," Donna said. "I had a spoon made I want you to try. Here." She handed Jenny a deep spoon with a special easy-to-grasp handle. "Use the spoon with your good hand, and hold this pusher in your right. Eat."

Jenny took the cutlery and after a few tries managed to get some spaghetti onto the spoon. She lifted the food to her mouth, but before it got there all the spaghetti fell into her lap. "Now see what you've done!"

"I didn't do it," Donna said, trying to hide a smile.

"Don't you laugh at me! Don't you dare."

"I am not laughing, Jenny. But you have to give it a few tries. Keep at it."

"Damn, damn. . . ." Close to tears as the same thing happened the second time, and the third, Jenny yelled, "I don't want any of this. To hell with it!" With a sweep of her arm she knocked the plate of food to the floor. "I'm like all the other cripples here. I can't feed myself; I can't do anything. So I might as well become just like them—eat like an animal and throw my food on the floor." She hurled the tray down and wheeled herself furiously out the door.

In her room, Jenny got herself out of the wheelchair and into bed, where she pulled the covers over her head. She lay in bed, panting with exhaustion, too angry to cry, furious with the whole world.

She was still quivering when Sally came into her room. "Okay, Jenny," Sally said, standing above her, "come out of hiding and let's talk about it."

"There's nothing to talk about," Jenny said in a muffled voice.

"I think there is." Gently Sally drew the covers

back and pulled up a chair next to the bed. "You don't like spaghetti?"

"It's ridiculous to give a bunch of cripples something like that to eat. Stupid."

"The kids happen to love it. They have a wonderful time."

"It's disgusting."

"To watch a bunch of kids enjoy themselves, forget their handicaps and try to feed themselves? On the contrary, I think it's pretty wonderful. I think it's sad to see someone with a lot of guts give up."

"I don't feel like listening to a lecture."

"Sorry, I don't mean to be lecturing. But snap out of it, Jenny. You're going to make a lot of messes before you're through. You're going to spill food, drop things, be awkward, have a million little frustrations learning how to make your limbs work. But if you don't keep at it, you never will learn. If you're lazy and impatient, you may remain crippled. If you work at it, though, your chances are better than even that you won't. It's your decision."

Sally got up and said good-night. Jenny heard Lanie come in, but she pretended she was asleep. Sally's words had frightened her. As much as she had talked about the possibility that she would remain crippled, Jenny had never really believed she would.

That couldn't happen to her. She had always recovered before from any illness, and she'd get well again. But Sally's matter-of-fact words had penetrated more deeply than the vague statements of the doctors. "If you're lazy and impatient. . . ." That her recovery might actually be up to her was also something Jenny had not quite believed. Doctors were the ones who made people well. What could a kid like Jenny Melino do? Lying in bed that night, Jenny made up her mind that she would have to find out.

For the rest of the week Jenny spent every morning in the occupational-therapy room, trying to pick up small colored blocks with her right hand. They were of different shapes, and Jenny was to drop each block into a matching compartment. Her progress was uneven. "You just have to keep at it," Donna, the occupational therapist, told her. When she managed to get a block in place, Jenny was jubilant.

Other times, when a block fell out of her hand, she hurled them all to the floor. After a few such fits, Jenny realized that no one scolded her. No one even paid attention. By the end of the week, Jenny's performance had improved. She was getting more blocks into place than not.

On Sunday her mother appeared with Mike and

Kate. Jenny was very excited about seeing them and eager to tell her mother about the progress she had made with her hand and arm. Of course, she was still in a wheelchair and her leg was still useless, but she felt encouraged. However, Kate immediately started to talk about school, and then Mike told her about a ball game (he was on the team), and Jenny found she didn't have a chance to tell them anything at all.

Kate had put a package down on the bureau, and after a while she said, "I brought you some candy. Should I open it?"

"Sure," Jenny said.

Kate handed the box of assorted chocolates to Mrs. Melino. "Here, have some."

"I'll pick one out for Jenny, too," Mrs. Melino said. "What do you want, hard or soft?"

"I can take my own," Jenny said, grabbing the chance to show off her hard-won accomplishment. She bent over the box and slowly lifted her right arm, trying to pick up a piece of candy. The other three watched her as if she was crossing a high wire in the circus. Finally she lodged a chocolate between her fingers, and she was carrying it up to her mouth when it fell to the floor.

Kate looked embarrassed and turned away with tears in her eyes. Mrs. Melino stooped to pick up the candy. Gruffly Mike took another piece of candy out of the box and handed it to Jenny. "Here."

"But I did it. I did it all week with blocks. Give me the box. I'm going to try again." Jenny looked at them defiantly.

"Maybe it's easier with blocks," Mike said, moving about nervously, obviously unwilling to watch Jenny go through another attempt.

"She has to try," Mrs. Melino said gently, handing Jenny the box.

Again Jenny managed to grasp a piece of candy and bring it slowly up to her mouth. This time she popped the whole piece in. "See," she said proudly, "it didn't fall down."

The three faces turned toward her didn't reflect her pleasure. Her mother seemed anxious, Kate looked even more embarrassed, and Mike was frankly unimpressed. His scowl clearly said, "Is that all they've done for you here?"

Jenny felt a wall between them and her. She became even more depressed after they left. They're absolutely right, she thought miserably. What's the big deal in taking a piece of candy out of a box?

Jenny sat hunched in her wheelchair and wondered why she had felt so good before her mother and Mike and Kate had come. Everything is out of proportion in this damn place, she thought. I'm getting to be as cuckoo as the rest of them.

She was not in a good mood when Donna popped in and said cheerily, "Did you show off to your mother?"

Jenny didn't answer. Then she yelled, "No. There's nothing to show off."

"What's the matter with you?"

"Nothing. Nothing at all. I'm just dandy. I'm just sitting in this chair because it's so pretty. Do you think it will go in my bedroom?" Jenny scowled at the therapist.

Donna came into the room and sat down on Jenny's bed. "What happened? Tell me, please."

"I showed how smart I am. After dropping candy on the floor, I did manage to pick up a piece and land it in my mouth. Don't you think I should get a gold medal? My brother thought it was simply marvelous. The others did too. Oh, boy, were they impressed. They couldn't wait to get out of here, watching me was so disgusting."

"Oh, Jenny, someone should have warned you. I'm so sorry. I feel terrible. . . ."

"Why should you feel terrible? You can pick up specks of dust with either hand any time you please."

"That is not the point. I'm sorry because your

128

brother's reaction—your mother's too—happens all the time. They simply don't understand. They don't know all the work that goes into relearning how to use parts of your body. You've made so much progress this week that I hate to see you discouraged."

"A week to pick up a piece of candy. How many weeks or months to use a knife and fork, to comb my hair, to button my clothes, to tie a shoelace, to write my name? What's the use?"

"You know the answer as well as I do." Donna stood up. "It's your life. You can handle it any way you want." Donna's eyes were softer than her voice, but she quickly walked out of the room.

Jenny got herself into bed and was lying with her eyes closed when Lanie came in. She had left early to go out with her mother, whom Jenny had not met. Now she was accompanied by a handsome woman and a man in a chauffeur's uniform. The chauffeur was carrying a couple of large boxes. "Just put them down on the bed," Lanie said. "Thanks, Roger. Mom, you'll have to open them. I can't."

"Of course, darling." Mrs. Fitzpatrick spoke in low, cultured tones.

Lanie swung around so that she could see Jenny. "Are you awake?"

"Yes." Jenny kept looking at Lanie's mother.

Lanie introduced her mother and Roger. Mrs. Fitzpatrick came over to Jenny, bent down, and gave her a light kiss on the cheek. "Lanie's told me all about you. I'm so glad she has you for a roommate. It makes her being here so much easier."

"I'm glad to have her, too," Jenny said.

When Mrs. Fitzpatrick and her chauffeur left, Jenny turned to Lanie. "You never told me you were so rich. You might have let me know." Still grouchy, she knew she was looking for a fight.

"Why?" Lanie's eyes were wide with surprise. "What difference does it make? We're not million-aires."

"You must be pretty rich to have a chauffeur. Does he drive a limousine?"

"He drives whatever car my mother wants to use. She doesn't drive and refuses to learn how."

"Whatever car she wants to use? How many cars have you got?" Jenny's voice revealed her outrage.

"As a matter of fact, we have four cars. My mother has two fur coats, a necklace worth about ten thousand dollars, and I have a trust fund left me by my grandmother. You're being ridiculous, Jenny," Lanie said coldly.

"Oh, sure. You rich people are all alike. You think it's vulgar to talk about money. I know girls like you in my class, so holier-than-thou. Cocky, stuck-up, talking about the museums they visited on their trips to Europe and the awful poverty in India or Mexico or wherever the hell they went for their fancy vacations. Being so smart and intellectual when it all boils down to having rich daddies. I'd be smart too if I went to all those places, smarter than they are."

Lanie just stared at Jenny throughout her outburst. "You really are mad, aren't you?"

"You're right I'm mad. It was one of your kind that got me into this mess, and now I have you for a roommate. It's too much."

"If you want to hate me just because I happen to have a rich father, that's your business. But I can't think of anything stupider."

"Don't flatter yourself that I hate you. I don't have that strong a feeling for you." Jenny closed her eyes and turned her head. She'd made one mess after another all day. Damn Adam DeWitt. She wished she'd never laid eyes on him.

11

Adam walked into the reception hall at Hilltop with a small knot of apprehension in his stomach. He purposely had not let Jenny know he was coming. He wanted to take her by surprise. Anyway, she might have told him not to come. For reassurance, Adam patted the large, flat package under his arm, the photograph of Jenny with the first-prize blue ribbon he had won in the art exhibit attached to it.

He found Jenny in the recreation room, sitting in a corner reading. She hadn't expected to see him, but she did give him a smile.

"Do we have to stay here?" Adam gestured toward the room full of noisy children.

"We could go to my room. No one's there; my roommate is out."

Adam walked alongside the wheelchair to Jenny's room. "I was afraid you might still be mad at me," he said, moving about the room restlessly while Jenny wheeled herself over toward the window.

"I have been. But I guess it's stupid to be angry. What's done is done."

"I have something for you." Adam tore the paper off the picture and held it up for Jenny to see. There she was, on her skates, her body half turned to face the camera, a slight smile on her face. The background, soft and misty, made the figure stand out sharply.

Jenny gasped and stared silently at the photograph for several minutes. "You are about the stupidest person I have ever known." She spoke in a slow, deliberate voice. "You could go to Harvard for a million years, and you still wouldn't know anything. Just wrap that thing up and take it away. Fast."

"What on earth is the matter? It's a marvelous

picture, the best I ever did. It won first prize. I thought you'd like to have it."

"You thought crazy. Do you think I want to look at that? Just look at me. *Look at me.* Look at my legs. That's a picture of someone else. Someone I don't even remember. I don't want a picture of a stranger. Take it away." She wasn't yelling. She was still speaking in a quiet, tired voice.

Adam came over and stood in front of her, the picture in his hand. "You're wrong, Jenny. The picture *is* you. It has nothing to do with anyone skating or walking. That's why it won first prize. The judges said so. It's a picture of a person, a personality, someone with spirit, a love of life. It's you, and it'll always be you."

"It's not, it's not." She was yelling at him now. "I don't love life. I hate it. I don't want to live if I'm going to be a cripple. I hate living this way."

Adam took both her hands in his. "I don't believe you. I believe the girl in the picture; that's you. You're not going to give up. You just aren't."

Jenny pulled her hands away. "Don't you give me any pep talk. That's too much coming from you. Just leave me alone. Go off to Harvard and your Honda. I don't know why you came to see me . . . and to bring me this picture. It's too much."

134

"I'm not going to Harvard, and I'm getting rid of the Honda. It's up for sale. I don't want it. I'm sorry you don't like the picture, but you're making a mistake. It is you, and you're still the same girl, and you always will be. Just look at that picture, and you'll know why I wanted to get to know you."

"I don't care why. I wish you hadn't."

"Listen, I'm going to leave the picture here. You can do what you want with it. I won't come see you again unless you ask me. Just call me and I'll come." He propped the portrait up on her bureau, gave her a kiss before she could stop him, and left.

The fresh air outside felt good. He probably hadn't been with Jenny long, yet Adam felt he had accomplished something. Her anger hadn't hurt the way it had before, and he felt a confidence about the picture. She would *have* to see what it showed so clearly, what he had wanted to capture in the many shots he had taken of her: her spirit, her love of life. If she recognized that, she'd be okay. Adam was surprised that he felt so confident, but one thing he felt sure of was his photography.

Adam was right. Everyone who came into Jenny's room stopped to admire the photograph. "It sure is you," Lanie said repeatedly.

Sally was the only one to whom Jenny confided her feelings. "It *was* me, but I'm not that girl anymore. I was furious when he brought the picture to me."

"You shouldn't have been. He was absolutely right." Sally laughed. "Even when you're angry you have the same spirit. Sure you get discouraged here—it's only natural—but you can fight if you let yourself. I know it."

"My mother's a fighter. I never liked that about her. I always wanted to be different—quiet and refined."

"Refinement goes deeper than how you speak. People like you and me have to struggle to get what we want. No one's going to hand it to us. But that doesn't make us coarse or vulgar. We still have to fight."

"I'm finding that out," Jenny said.

She wouldn't have called it "fighting," but she knew what Sally meant. Jenny was doing it in the swimming pool when she kicked with her legs ten, sometimes twenty, times more than she had to, when she was in the physical-therapy room and worked without stopping at her leg exercises, in occupational therapy where she used her fingers until they ached.

The day came when Lanie's mother arrived, packed

Lanie's things, and took her home. "Of course, we'll see each other," Lanie said, but Jenny knew better. Lanie didn't understand that she and Jenny lived in different worlds. Jenny was sorry—she had grown to like Lanie—but what mattered to her now was whether Fred, the physical therapist, thought she was moving her leg a little better. All the longings and resentments she had felt became insignificant. Her thoughts and energy were concentrated on getting better.

Jenny badgered Sally, who got reports of her progress, constantly. "What did they say? Am I improving? Will I be able to walk?"

"You're working hard, Jenny," she answered one day. "We're all proud of you. Just keep at it." Sally laughed. "Keep looking at that picture Adam took; he had the right idea."

"But will I walk?"

Sally's face turned serious. "No one really knows how well you'll walk. I'm going to be honest with you. You may have a limp. It's hard to say. But that shouldn't hamper you."

Jenny paled. "A limp . . . what kind of limp?"

"I said we don't know. You may not. Jenny, don't start dwelling on that. I just wanted you to be prepared in case. . . ."

137

"How does one prepare oneself to be a cripple?" Jenny asked bleakly.

Sally bent over and hugged her. "Don't think about it. Just keep on working."

Jenny did keep on working, and several weeks later reached another milestone in her session with Fred. After he manipulated her leg several times, he said, "Listen, I'm going to support you under your arms and get you to stand up. Then we'll see what weight you can put on your leg. Now just let me help you stand up."

Slowly Fred pulled her up till she was standing. "Can you move your right leg forward, as if you were going to take a step?" he asked.

"I think so," Jenny said nervously. She moved her leg, just a little, and for a second or two she let her weight rest on it. Then she grabbed hold of Fred.

"Stand on your two feet. Just stand still." He disengaged himself and let her stand alone. "See, you're doing it!" She wavered, and he grabbed her, but she didn't fall.

"Okay, come on. We're going to take another step," Fred said. With his help Jenny walked about four or five steps before Fred let her sink down on the mattress.

"That was pretty classy, wasn't it? See, you did it even without a walker, didn't you?" Fred looked at her proudly.

Jenny was exhausted, but she had a wide smile on her face. "I guess that was classy," she said. "What made you say classy? That's a funny word to use."

Fred shrugged. "It's a good word when someone does something elegant, just right. Your body moved right, Jenny, and to me that's classy. You rest a few minutes, and then we'll do your exercises."

Jenny stared at her legs stretched out in front of her. "I walked," she said with wonder. "I really did walk, didn't I?" She turned up her face to Fred.

"Yes, my dear, you did walk."

Even after she left Fred, Jenny kept thinking about what had happened. It was nothing like what she had imagined would happen. Ever since she had arrived at Hilltop she had thought about the time when she would get up from her wheelchair and surprise everyone by walking. In her mind she changed the time and place; sometimes she thought she would do it casually when her mother was there; other times she thought she would surprise all the doctors in the middle of a consultation. Dr. Hayes was in charge of her case, and he would be especially surprised. She had also fantasized calmly walking into Sally's office one day. In a way, the reality of being alone with Fred had been an anticlimax. But it *had* happened; she had walked. Jenny thought about it all day and couldn't wait for her mother to come that evening, her night off.

"I really did walk," Jenny said to her mother. "Of course, Fred helped me. I mean I didn't just get up and take off, but I managed very well. Fred said I was classy." Jenny examined her legs, stretched out in front of her on her bed. "They're pretty skinny, aren't they?"

"You have to get your muscle tone back," her mother said.

"I know. But I think I'll be able to come home soon, don't you?"

"We'll have to see what the doctor says. I imagine you'll need a lot of therapy. I almost forgot to tell you, Mike got his driver's license. He said he's going to drive over to see you very soon."

"Terrific. Then if they let me go home, Mike could bring me in for therapy if I need it. So you wouldn't have to do it." Jenny looked pleased.

"We'll have to see," Mrs. Melino repeated.

"Mom, I want to tell you something, but don't tell Mike."

Mrs. Melino looked at Jenny anxiously. "What is it?"

"If I can walk and am okay, Adam needn't feel so badly, need he?"

"He can't undo what you've gone through. Don't worry about Adam."

"I think about him. He helped me, you know." Jenny directed her mother to open her bottom bureau drawer. She had put the photograph away so her mother and Mike wouldn't see it.

Mrs. Melino gasped. "Oh, Jenny. . . ." Her eyes filled with tears.

"I know. I felt the same way. I was pretty mad when he brought it. But the picture helped me. It's hard to explain, but. . . . Well, I'm the same girl who's in that picture, and at the same time I'm different. I mean, all that energy I had, I still have it, but I'm using it differently. I have to plan everything. I hated it at first—planning how to get dressed or get in and out of bed. But now those things are easier. I plan my time, whether I want to spend more time swimming or reading. I feel more in control. Does that sound crazy to you?"

"No, darling. It sounds very grown-up."

Jenny dismissed that approval with a wave of her hand. "I want to show Adam I can walk."

"You walk for yourself, not Adam," her mother said.

"Of course," Jenny agreed, but she knew that it was very important to show Adam that she could walk.

12

Jenny sat in Dr. Hayes' office and waited for him to come in. Through the window she watched the wind blow across a tall, yellow-leafed maple and send the leaves falling gracefully to the ground. It was a little over ten weeks since Jenny had come to Hilltop. Earlier that day she had been given another neurological examination by a visiting consultant, and Dr. Hayes was to tell her the results.

143

"Well, young lady, how are you?" Dr. Hayes' voice boomed as he came bustling into the room. He dropped a briefcase on the desk and sat down and faced her.

"I've got some good news for you," he said jovially. "We're going to try you on a walker. Don't expect miracles; you're going to feel wobbly. Try not to take any spills. You're not going to start walking all of a sudden, you know. It's a slow process, and you'll need to take your time. I'll let them know down in physical therapy. Then, I'll see you in a few days." He dismissed her with a curt nod.

He was so matter-of-fact. How could he be so calm, telling her such fantastic news? Jenny wanted to get up and shout, to run, to do something to express her excitment. "Can you lend me a dime?" she asked the doctor.

He looked at her with surprise and rummaged through his pocket. "Yes, I guess so. Whatever for?"

"I want to call my mother and tell her. I'm too excited to go all the way back to my room for money."

Dr. Hayes handed her the dime with a laugh. "That's a good reason. You don't have to give it back to me. But remember what I told you. Take it slowly."

Jenny phoned her mother and told her the good

news. "I bet I'll be out of here in no time," she said. "You'll see."

"Do be careful." Mrs. Melino sounded just like the doctor. "Take it slowly; don't be impatient."

Jenny wished she'd borrowed another dime. There was another call she wanted to make before she could change her mind. She wanted to talk to Adam. She saw Sally coming down the hall and rushed out to tell her the news.

"That's marvelous, Jenny. I'm so happy for you." Sally's reaction was more satisfactory.

"Have you got a dime you could lend me?" Jenny asked.

"You want to call your mother?"

"I just did. No, I want to call someone else." Jenny felt herself blushing.

Sally laughed. "Your boyfriend?" She handed her a dime.

"Kind of. Maybe," Jenny said.

Jenny's heart was hammering as she dialed Adam's number, and she prayed that he would answer the phone. She didn't want to speak to his mother. With relief, she heard Adam's voice say, "Hello."

"Adam, this is Jenny. Yes, Jenny. I'm good. I can't talk long because I'm in a phone booth. Yes, sure, I'm at Hilltop. Say, do you want to come to see me?

I don't care, whenever you like. Over the weekend is best. I'm always here. Come as soon as you want. I think my dime's running out. Good-bye."

Jenny felt breathless when she hung up the receiver, as though she had just accomplished some exhausting physical ordeal, but she was very happy that she had gone ahead and made the call.

Adam did not appear on Saturday, and Sunday found Jenny restlessly waiting for him. The excitement of her walker had worn off. She felt clumsy using it, and she was still dragging her right leg. The wheelchair had been much faster and less tiring. Dr. Hayes had told her that she would have to continue exercising her legs to make them strong, but he had made no promises about her walking perfectly. Jenny had set herself a goal of walking up and down the hall five additional times each day. Yesterday she had made fifteen trips, and today it was going to be twenty.

She was on her fourteenth round when Adam appeared at the end of the hall. He had a small bunch of flowers in his hand, which he handed to her solemnly. He glanced at the walker uneasily. "Are you going to have to use that thing for walking?"

146

"No, silly. This is a great step forward from the wheelchair. I asked you to come so I could show off. I'm exercising my legs, walking this way. Don't you see?"

Adam looked relieved. "I thought you were going to be stuck with that. You look great anyway. Will you be coming out soon?"

"I don't know." Jenny led him slowly through the halls to her room.

Jenny settled in the one armchair, and Adam faced her, straddling a straight chair. Because he was looking at her with a puzzled expression, Jenny asked, "What's the matter?"

"You look different. I don't know how, but different."

"I am different. I'm not mad anymore. I wanted to tell you that picture you gave me really helped. I hated it at first, but I kept looking at it, and I decided that you were right. That girl really is me."

Adam grinned gratefully. "You're damn decent to tell me. Thanks."

"Anytime." Jenny laughed. "So here we are."

"Where are we?"

"I don't know. I guess we could be friends. . . . You're really not going to Harvard?"

"Not this fall. Maybe later. I feel stupid talking about my troubles to you. You've had enough to think about. But the accident got me thinking about a lot of things I took for granted before, like what's important and what isn't."

"I know." Jenny nodded. "Here some little things became important. Who'd ever have thought that being able to hold a fork could matter more than anything else?"

"It's important when you can't do it. My going to Harvard maybe is more important to your brother Mike than it is to me. You know what I mean?"

"You can go and he can't?"

"Exactly. How is he by the way? Still so mad at me?"

"I guess so. Do you care?"

Adam got up and started to walk about the room. "I think I do, but less than before. I'm beginning to figure out why. His feelings really have nothing to do with me as a person, but what he thinks I stand for. It's his problem, not mine. But I don't want to talk about Mike."

"You brought him up. What do you want to talk about?"

"You. Can I ask you a direct question?"

148

"You can try."

Adam looked at her steadily. "What's the prognosis? Are you going to walk again?"

Jenny returned his gaze unflinchingly. "They don't know yet. It looks as though I'll be able to walk, but I may have a limp."

Adam turned away, and Jenny thought he might be trembling. Then he faced her again. "Jenny, is there anything you need or want? *Anything* I can do? We've got to be honest with each other. At least I have money. . . ."

"I know you have." She spoke quietly. "There's nothing you can do, Adam. That's one of the things that's happened to me. I used to think that money could do anything, protect people, keep them safe. But it doesn't work that way, does it?"

"Safe, no. There is no real safety, is there?"

"But you don't *have* to walk under ladders," Jenny said and laughed.

"Or ride on motorcycles," Adam muttered.

Jenny held out her arms to him. She had a great desire to touch him, to hold him.

He turned to go to her when the door opened and Mike came in. He stopped when he saw Adam. "I'll come back later," he mumbled.

149

"You can stay. Mike, please, Adam's my friend."

"He's not mine. I'd just as soon not be here when he is. Besides, I told him to stay away from you. He's no friend to you, Jenny. . . ."

"Why don't you shut up and behave yourself? If I'm not mad at Adam, you don't have to be."

"If you had any sense, you'd have nothing to do with him. I don't know how you can stand even to look at him."

Adam, who had been standing quietly looking from one to the other, picked up his jacket. "I'll go, Jenny. I'll come back another time."

"Not if I can help it," Mike threatened.

"Mike, be quiet. I'll decide who can come to see me, not you. I'm sick of you going around with a chip on your shoulder and using my accident as an excuse. You want a lot of things you don't have, but that's not Adam's fault. Get wise to yourself."

Mike looked at his sister in surprise. "You want them just as much as I do. You're always looking at those fashion magazines and mooning about the stuff you'd like to have, trying to fix our house up. . . . You're no different."

"Maybe not, but at least I don't go around blaming someone else for my life."

"I'm going," Adam said. "I'll see you soon," he said to Jenny.

"Come back whenever you want."

Adam left, and Mike looked at Jenny unhappily. "I suppose you're mad because I sent him away."

"I don't get mad so easily anymore. But I think you're stupid to act that way about Adam."

"It's the way I feel, that's all. I just don't like him."

"I don't care if you do or you don't, but stop bugging me about him. He's my friend, and as he said, it's your problem if you don't like him, not his."

"He said that, did he?"

"Yes, he said that. And he's right, Mike. Think about it." Jenny closed her eyes. The emotional strain of seeing Adam and now dealing with Mike's anger was tiring.

"You want to go to sleep?"

"No, but I'm a little tired."

"I'm sorry if I got you upset about Adam. I'll stop bugging you, but try to keep him out of my way. Okay?"

"Okay. I probably won't be seeing so much of him anyway. Even if he doesn't go to Harvard."

"Why wouldn't you?"

"I like Adam, but I don't *need* him anymore."

"What did you ever need him for?"

Jenny looked at her brother through half-closed eyes. "It's too much to explain. Maybe for the same reason you don't like him."

Mike gave her a shrewd glance. "You thought he'd introduce you to some millionaires?"

Jenny laughed. "Something like that. It seems a long time ago. Anyway, if I do walk with a limp, he'll be feeling sorry for me, and I couldn't stand that."

"Is that how it's going to be?" Mike asked sharply.

"They don't know, but it's possible."

"You sound awfully calm about it."

"What can I do? I've been working hard to get my legs stronger, and I'll keep on. But there are some things you have to accept whether you like them or not." Jenny's face said that she didn't want to talk about the future anymore.

"You think you'll come home soon?"

"I hope so."

"It's been lonesome without you."

"It's lonesome here, too. Give me the news."

"Nothing much," Mike said, which was what he always said. Jenny rested her head against the chair and pictured her room and their house, the neighbors on her street. They all looked good to her, and she knew that when she got home, her time in the hospital eventually would fade into the background. Even the pain and the boredom would become a blur. . . .

"If you were going to paint your room, what color would you do it?" Mike asked, elaborately casual.

Jenny grinned. "Are you painting my room?"

"I didn't say that. I'm just asking a question."

"I think all white. Maybe one wall yellow, the one away from the windows. Mike, that's terrific."

"Don't expect anything," Mike said, but he was grinning. "Just hurry up and come home."

"What do you think I'm doing? It should be pretty soon," Jenny said. "My legs are getting stronger every day."

After Mike left, Jenny thought about going home. It was going to be odd, leaving the routine of the hospital and going back to a normal life. Here everyone was concerned with their latest lab test or examination, with getting mail and visitors, with a date for going home. It was a separate, closed-in world. While Jenny was anxious to leave, she knew she would have to make a lot of adjustments to the world outside, especially if she was left with a limp. The hospital was safe, but as she and Adam had agreed, there was no absolute safety anywhere, not if you wanted to live. And of that wish Jenny was positive. Life was full of the unexpected, and perhaps that was what made it so exciting. She felt full of hope for the future; after such a streak of bad luck, something good was bound to happen.

Hila Colman was born and grew up in New York City, where she went to Calhoun School. After graduation, she attended Radcliffe College. Before she started writing for herself, she wrote publicity material and ran a book club. Her first story was sold to the *Saturday Evening Post*, and since then her stories and articles have appeared in many periodicals. Some have been dramatized for television. In 1957, she turned to writing books for teen-age girls. One of them, *The Girl From Puerto Rico*, was given a special citation by the Child Study Association of America.

Mrs. Colman lives in Bridgewater, Connecticut, and has two sons.